Cardiff 75

Contemporary Writing from the City

Cardiff 75

Contemporary Writing from the City

Edited by Sara Hayes, Paul Jauregui
and Martin Buckridge

Viridor and
Prosiect Gwyrdd
Community Fund

PARTHIAN

Parthian, Cardigan SA43 1ED
www.parthianbooks.com
ISBN 978-1-914595-40-0
© the contributors 2023
Edited by Carly Holmes
Cover design by Emily Courdelle
Typeset by Elaine Sharples www.typesetter.org.uk
Printed by 4edge Limited
Printed on FSC accredited paper

Foreword

It is my great privilege to have been chair of Cardiff Writers' Circle for seven years; especially in this our seventy-fifth birthday year. (No, I wasn't at the original meeting.) And many other local writing groups have joined with us to celebrate seventy-five years of creative writing in this city. We have held open mic evenings, a large writers' gathering at a city centre hotel, a seventy-five-word flash fiction competition, and a series of free tutorials presented by professional tutors, on many aspects of writing, presenting and publishing work. To cap this fantastic year off, and with our friends from the other groups, we are publishing this collection of seventy-five works, one for each year of creative writing in this fabulous city of the arts. Here you will find poetry, short stories, flash fiction, haiku; with almost every genre and style represented. We intend to continue this co-operation between groups with more projects and events, to encourage more people to take up their tablets, laptops, pens and paper, quills and vellum, whichever medium they prefer, and just get writing.

I hope you enjoy the works gathered here. And suggest you look out for the next collection – Cardiff 150.

Paul Jauregui
Chair of Cardiff Writers' Circle
October 2022

Preface

On 4 May 1947 eleven keen writers met in the Technical College in Park Place and agreed to launch Cardiff Writers' Circle. Seventy-five years on, the Circle is still active, the oldest continuously running creative writing group in Wales and one of the oldest in the UK. The group currently meets on Monday evenings at the YMCA in the aptly named Shakespeare Street off City Road, when we read and discuss our own work.

The Cardiff 75 project marks this anniversary, celebrating seventy-five years of creative writing in the city. Starting in July with a *Writers' Gathering* attended by local writers, publishers and speakers, other activities have included Saturday morning workshops and open mic sessions in the Flute and Tankard. Publication of this volume marks the final stage of the celebration.

Cardiff Writers' Circle is indebted to the many friends who have contributed time and energy to make connections between writing groups and support each other's writing.

Particular thanks go to Sharif Gemie who helped significantly in bringing this collection together. In addition, he has researched our records and interviewed members past and present to tell the story of our first 75 years in 'A History of the Cardiff Writers' Circle, 1947–2022', which can be downloaded free from:

https://cardiffwriterscircle.cymru/a-history-of-cardiff-writers-circle-1947-2022-by-sharif-gemie/

His short play written for the *Writers' Gathering*, '2022 to 1947 – A Backwards History', is included towards the end of this collection.

Cardiff 75 is a unique collection of seventy-five previously unpublished contemporary short stories and poems from the city. Contributors have diverse backgrounds and life experiences; they are from different writing groups or none. A few may be known to the reader, some have previously been published, others not. The common denominators that bring them together are a love of writing and a personal connection to Cardiff.

We are deeply grateful to our publishers Parthian and to Viridor and Prosiect Community Fund whose generous support has enabled production of this book.

Martin Buckridge
Sara Hayes
October 2022

Contents

CONTENTS

The Bone Layers

Winner of the Cardiff Writers' Circle
Short Story Competition 2022

Katherine Wheeler

It's hot. There's a stickiness to the air – half sweet, half threat – and the boys have come to join their fathers in the bone yard.

It is this time of the year that the boys age up from play fighting and class scuffles of their schools and take on a trade. There are many new apprentices who are donning their work coats and trowels for the first time.

It is easy to forget that construction is a job. It is mindless. It repeats layer upon layer. The mortar is mixed with sand and water, spooned onto the edge of a trowel and the mixture patted into an even paste, upon which the long bones will be placed. Many of the men stay until retirement, the grind of the day is something they can teach their hands. The callouses equalling trophies of their great and worthy work.

Everard's son is not used to the heat of the day and hides from the sky underneath his father's coat. Like the other boys, it is his first day. His clothes are ill-fitting, the cuffs hang past his fingertips and his boots slide loosely around his feet. He and his father have the job of hauling the bones from the stocks and placing them on top of the mortar. Everard's son will lay the corners, his father, the connecting walls.

"A corner piece is the most important of the house," says

his father. "For those, each part must be angled just so. It is the biggest job of them all."

The boy is given a piece to feel, to see how it weighs in his hands. It's light, easy enough to balance on the crux of a finger but weighty enough to shatter. The sweat on his palms is enough to slick the white until it shines against his skin. With it is a sensation, he feels it spinning around his head and ears. There's sickness in there, a sweet heady dancing of his thoughts.

He hands it back to his father, the surface leaving a white coating on his palms. The boy looks down at his arm, grabs around the flesh and to the harder tissue underneath. It is a straight line.

"How is it curvy?"

His father doesn't answer.

"I can bend sticks easy," the boy offers. "These are so powdery and weird."

"If you put it on right the first time, you won't have to adjust it. It dries fast. Look, I'll show you." The man scoops a trowel into the mortar and spreads a thick layer onto the bone. "Like this."

He places it down and the wall grows an inch higher.

"...and then you do it again?"

"Again and again. Until you have a house."

When the day is over, Everard's son walks along the docks. The sun hangs sharp orange fingers onto the horizon, its rays spread across the water. It is still hot outside; the scorching heat of a spring day burns the air. It is easier to breathe than earlier but the warmth still plants an ache in his throat.

He has never been this way before; it is a path reserved for only a few. It is usually empty, the ships along the water often deserted. Now he is learning a trade, he can walk where he is allowed. When the boy had peered in before, he had seen farmers, brandishing new tools and heavy bags behind them.

He walks for a while, counting ripples in the water, when the path stops. There is the left turn and a right – leading to the hay market and to the sea. The boy turns around, doubles back down the dockside path. He's gone too far to turn off so he follows the path beside the water's edge.

There's a ferry boat cruising past a small distance away. The boy squints at it. The captain is missing from the cab but there is a thin trail of steam from the funnel atop it. He stops, pausing until the boat passes the gleam of the sun, and looks again. The boat is large, the same brown as the waveless water. There's a square platform at the back populated by a group of silent figures. Some are lying on their sides, knees splayed out, folded into wordless L shapes. The others are bent, like they are caught in a bow. A few are walking from side to side, fingertips grazing and skimming the floor. They scutter wordlessly, unconscious of Everard's son, a few mad eyes darting to spots on the water.

He watches the boat cruise out of sight. The sun is nearly down and the water a drastic orange. When he walks here again, he'll watch out for the boat and the bent-double people.

Everard's son walks the path home and drinks the soup his mother gives him.

The next day is hotter than the first. It aches to move but the men in the bone yard stamp across the yard like tanks. The boy has been tasked with carrying the finer bones whilst his father does the heavy lifting. It is nothing-work, the kind he's already done in the schoolyard, but the ache of the daytime pierces through him. It is too hot. Too oppressive a day for being out in the open air. He slumps back against a heap of rubble and tips his head back...

One of the men screams from across the yard. The boy scrambles upright, scurrying to attention before the man seizes his arm.

"Keep moving, boy! For God's sake!" the man shouts. "Were you slouching?"

The boy squints at the question. A drop of sweat falls to the corner of this mouth and trickles down like spit. He looks around, his father is nowhere to be seen.

"Answer me!"

He looks back, up and then nods. "It's too hot. To work, sir."

"You will not slouch in the heat. Tomorrow you will carry the big bones."

The boy nods again. He will have to swallow the heat and keep moving.

When the day is over, he walks home along the docks to see the flat boat again but the water is empty and brown.

The third day it thunders. The yard is showered with tropical rain which hammers hard enough to pick the sand from the ground. The boy finds himself dragging his feet through puddles, the relative coolness of the water easing his scorched toes. He manages a steady pace, trying some of the bigger bones with less mortar this time. The walls of the house are getting bigger and for every side built up, there is another corner-piece to set. He handles two over the course of the day. The pieces are ridged, but set hard into right angles, like they would curl if they could. He remembers his father's instructions – a little mortar spread along the underside of the piece, laid down and left until set, you *must* measure the angle or the piece will go to waste.

"Well done," says one of the older men. "You learn fast. Too fast." He laughs, but the sound is tinged with a hollowness. A few of the other men join in, voices absent.

4

Everard's son thinks of the boat and its passengers. They hadn't noticed him, though the waterside was otherwise deserted. The boy wonders if they had been taking a ferry or ducking for a low bridge. Perhaps divers readying themselves for harbour swimming.

On the fourth day, he finishes a side by himself, sneaking a moment to rest out of sight where he can. The men make examples of themselves whilst he's looking: shoulders back, heads poised and knees bent when they lift. His father too, with a tight smile.

The fifth and sixth days go much the same, the walls building higher and higher until the men are working on ladders.

Everard's son notices his father sitting as they climb, basking in the shade of the workmen's cabin. He is not slouching. Is that why the men are not shouting? He has a drink too, the bluest liquid the boy has ever seen. His father looks peaceful, something he has rarely seen, his eyes lazily drooping open and closed. When the day ends, his father remains, a lazy smile on his face and the drink drained.

He walks home along the docks again. It's as hot as it was the first day he arrived, the sun distorting the brown water as it peeks over the horizon. He's halfway home when he notices that he's not alone.

Up ahead, there's a team of haulers perched on the water's edge. They look rough and weather worn. Some are smoking long pipes, others cramming large wads of bread into their mouths. A flat ferry boat bobs up and down beside them, tethered to the shore, the very same he had seen before. This time, there are large tubs of blue fluid strapped to the back, strung tightly with binding ropes and plastered with foreign looking labels.

As he approaches, one of the haulers looks up and flashes him a weary smile. "A landlubber!"

The boy stops, smiles, opens his mouth and then closes it again. A few of the other men glance round to where he is standing, their jaws grinding on bread and tobacco. "Are you the ferrymen?" he asks.

"We do any an' all sorts," says the man. "We're waitin' up. Special delivery. They're closin' up dock soon, so we can get out safe an' all that."

The boy glances over the boat's cargo. There are stickers the whole way around showing symbols he's never seen before. "What are you carrying?"

The man with the smile sniffs and picks up a bottle from beside him. "Med'cin. 'Elps people stay still when they fidgetin'. Yer too young for that so don't you be thinkin' about it, ey?"

Some of the men turn back towards the water, he can hear their heavy breaths from a distance.

"I saw people on the boat. All bent and touching their toes. Are they divers?"

The man's smile slips for a second. Everard's son can see the lines on the man's face thicken as he repairs it.

"They were jus' getting' from one place to another. Stretchin'. Retired folks. Stayin' like that. It's good for 'em."

A few of the other men spare glances at the two of them, their eyes tired. The boy frowns.

"I get told off for slouching."

The man's smile fails. He raises his bottle towards the path out.

"The dock is closin' up. I'd get yerself out. We got folks to put on board."

On the seventh day, the boy arrives late to the yard. The air is scorching, burning the ground beneath the site. Despite it, the men are ploughing through. They are nearly at the top of the wall now, the sides forming a square.

He keeps moving, stamping down the dirt of the yard as he walks. The bones are cool to the touch today and they soothe like balm when he touches them. The boy starts with the corner-piece and climbs with it tucked snugly under his arm. He is growing to like the strange bones and their ridges.

As he reaches the top of the ladder, he glances over at the entranceway. There, planted in the dirt are his father's boots. Only, when Everard's son looks again, his father is bent in two. His hands graze the floor, tracing the sand as the wind sways him. The boy opens his mouth just as his father looks up, chin coated in blue, eyes glazed with a haze of white. His body, his calloused body is folded to a corner. Everard's son looks down at the bone in his hand —

Heartbuzz

Saoirse Anton

A side step, wide step,
keep your distance stance
choreography of change
in our cautious daily dance.
It feels a step too far
from where we are at home
when no easy closeness keeps us
grounded through this storm.

But as the unknown swarms
a warm little buzz,
a pollen covered fuzz,
catches my ear and eye
and looking to my left I see,
nose in nectar nestled,
a bustling bumblebee.

No world-weary worry
weighs down these
busy wings,
as this bee buzzing sings a
song of honey-sweetness.

And with the sound of her song
I'm no longer in a
virus ridden, hunger bitten
news cycle circus world but
in this moment that unfurled
from the pollen heavy
petals of a flower.

In this bumble-industry
there is a stillness
as the storm spreads, relentless
outside the fleeting floral calm which
reassures.

One glance left
and I'm reminded,
that the world is turning,
deftly twirling in
the dance it always has.

Our choreography of change
will change again
to match new rhythm or refrain,
and when it does,
I'll hear the echo of a little buzz
and know the heart beats on the same.

Silver Laces

Nisha Harichandran

Arms crossed, Kevin smirks, *'There's more than one, hon. Cut them all?'* *'No, just the front, please.'* Kevin schedules a follow-up and waves me out. Puffing, my shoulders tense. I guess eloquence is not for all. But then, there wasn't anything wrong with what he said. Kev was being direct. So, why and what am I choosing to hide? As thoughts percolate, the antique mirror catches my eye. Pausing, I check myself out and continue onto the main road, strutting like a peacock, flicking between smiles and frowns, whilst the freshly set curls kiss each cheek with equal affection.

Love a day at the salon. Best forty-five minutes and clears my head instantly. The few seconds of quiet evaporate at the sound of her voice. *'Michele! It's me, Jessica!'* Gliding the escalator like a swan on heels, she strides towards me, flaunting her ring finger. *'Sealed it!'* She buries me in a hug. I give in awkwardly, for my hair's sake. *'Long time. How are you? Married?'* I shuffle towards the exit. *'All good. Just back from a conference. Glad for the bank holiday weekend.'* Flapping her hands, she fusses, mocking my response. I squint, the diamonds dizzying my vision. *'Always talking about work. Clock's ticking, babe. Kiss some frogs. One'll be a prince!'* Stroking my hair pitifully, she whispers, *'They show. Can't hide behind the highlights. Trust me, babe.'* I'd rather sky-jump than trust you babe, I wanted to scream but faked a smile instead.

My eyes drift to thoughts of college days, travels abroad, and then to the fluttering pages on my coffee table. Marked in bold, the quote reads, *'Not everyone has the opportunity to grow old.'* That's bloody right. My silver laces are a privilege. Richard Gere oozes sexiness in his salt and pepper; I darn sure can rock mine. These laces witnessed my growth and supported my ambitions. I am keeping them.

Sauntering in, Kevin greets me, *'Right on time hon. Cappuccino?'* *'Yes, please.'* *'The usual today? Root touch-up?'* *'Yes'.* *'See a few whites, hon. Take them off?'* *'Nope. Let them blend in.'*

Mermaid Quay

Leusa Lloyd

I remember the days
When we lived in Cathays,
And we'd slip away to Mermaid Quay,
We'd drink down the docks –
JD on the rocks –
Singing songs of the plays we'd seen,

We'd walk to Penarth,
Hang our socks by the hearth,
Hot toddies until the flu passed.
We'd explore the Arcades,
That slink round like a maze,
As we soaked up the sun, we laughed.

Back at the Bay,
The Basin was black,
Clouds threatened attack,
And the currents were rough.
Back at the Bay,
You asked me to stay,
But I said this wasn't enough.

Stricken with doubt,
At the jetty, I looked out,
On my tongue the taste of the sea,
Alone, at last, my tears flowed free,
My head a penitentiary,
Playing a fading memory:
Your kiss on my lip,
Your hand on my hip,
Your palm in my grip...

Oh, how the whole world would glitter for me,
When we danced round Mermaid Quay.

Sand and Foam

(West Wales, November 1956)

Sharif Gemie

Sometimes, at low tide, I find cockle-pickers, bent over in their waders, scrabbling in the wet sand. Sometimes, on sunny days, I see day-trippers arrive. They hold picnics on the grassy banks and their children build sandcastles and run along the shore, shrieking and laughing. But sometimes, like on this grey November afternoon, there's no one. I walk over the glistening grey-blue sand and admire the ornamentation stretching out before me: reflections of clouds, sky and moments of sun. It's as if I can walk to the horizon and beyond. Blake found infinity in a grain of sand, I glimpse it in this mad meeting of sand, sea and sky. I walk and walk, and I forget London and my wife and my work, I forget Eden and Nasser, I forget Suez and Hungary, I forget everything, just let it all dissolve in the swirling sea-breezes and the shimmering grey. My head empties, my limbs freeze, my lungs fill and something heals inside me.

But I can't float away into this grey infinity. Two chains bind me to the earth: the time of the tide and the hour of sunset. As the blue of the sea turns a dimmer blue-grey, I turn round, trudge back across the glistening sand and I realise I'm no longer alone. There's a white dot on the quayside. Each step brings me closer and new details emerge. A white square and a blue line – a canvas and a painter. What madman would paint this view today? A blue scarf, flapping in the wind. An arm raised, then falling. A cap. My God, it's a woman. Not young, but – it's hard to be sure, she's wrapped up like a trooper in an old khaki greatcoat.

'Afternoon!' she calls out. 'A study in grey, has to be, doesn't it?'

She grins, white teeth flashing above her sky-blue scarf.

For a moment, I'm stunned. I'm frozen by the wind and I can't think what to say.

She looks at her painting, dabs at it with her brush, hums a little.

'Getting colder.' She glances at me.

I have to speak. 'You've – you've chosen an odd view. It's all grey.'

I feel a stab of guilt. How can I betray my glimpse of infinity with these trite words? But I must keep it to myself, I can't tell her, she mustn't know.

'I like a challenge.'

'You're from London?' I ask.

'Of course. Had to get away.'

I edge round to see her canvas and feel relieved that it's just a seaside view, perhaps greyer than normal. She's exaggerated the sunlight, decorated the sand with specks of gold.

'Hmmm?' she asks.

I nod.

She stands back, head to one side, assessing her own work.

'Had to get away,' she repeats. 'Couldn't face one more newspaper headline or wireless broadcast. Suez!' She rolls her eyes. 'Sometimes people are so stupid, aren't they? Nobody *does* anything, nobody knows what to do.'

I nod once more. What certainty! It's refreshing.

'Still…' she sighs. 'Politics, eh? I said I wanted to get away from it.'

'Everyone's affected, I suppose.' Somehow it sounds like I'm apologising. 'It's everywhere.'

'Hah!'

She wipes her brush on a multi-coloured cloth, stares at her canvas.

'It's not finished,' she says. 'I'll come back tomorrow.'

She packs up her paints and easel and slips them into one of those tartan shopping trolleys that housewives use for their weekly shop. The canvas perches on top.

'Georgina.' She holds out her hand. 'Or Georgie, if you must.'

'Edmund.'

We shake hands.

'I'm here for the Creative Writing course. In town.' She gestures along the bay.

'You're a student?' I ask.

'No, I'm the tutor.'

'Really?'

'Do you write?'

'Not really, no.'

'Still, come along if you like. Every evening, this week. Listen to the others. Beginners welcome.' She smiles and steps towards me: she seems very close. 'It starts tonight, seven o'clock, in the church hall.'

'No, thank you, I won't, I've got to…'

My voice dies away. There's nothing I've got to do.

'Suit yourself.'

She walks towards the town, pulling her trolley behind her. It rattles along the uneven quayside. She stops, looks back at me.

'I'm staying over there.' I point the other way, up the hill to my little cottage.

'Right.'

At a quarter to seven, I decide to go to the church hall. At first, I hadn't wanted to, but I thought about my attempts to write poems and I remembered Georgina's smile over her blue scarf. I want to know more. What would she be like as a teacher? I've been alone for so long, barely speaking to a soul, staying by myself for days on end, I've turned into a hermit. I told my wife I'd be away for a week or two, but it had stretched into two months. I knew something was wrong, we both knew something was wrong, but neither of us were brave enough to name it. Why was she so awkward? Why couldn't she ever settle down to anything? Join in, just for once? Always changing, never certain, never agreeing. I knew it was difficult for her but, all the same... I couldn't help thinking she just wasn't trying. We'd exchanged a few letters. She told me our daughter was fine, I told her about the weather. She wrote that she was coping, running the bookshop by herself, I wrote that sales were never good in autumn. I knew there was another message, in between and behind our words, but I couldn't read it, or maybe I couldn't write it. And... it was easier to stay here and lose myself in the grey infinity of sand, sea and sky.

I shake my head, find the least scruffy of my two coats and set out.

The door to the church hall creaks as I push it open. I walk past a noticeboard with a week-old announcement of a public debate about 'The Crisis on the Nile'. Inside the musty hall, there's a half-circle of a dozen or so rickety chairs. People are sorting themselves out: stout, do-gooding ladies, blonde housewives, a couple of retired men in tweeds, a pale, thin young man who's trying to look like a poet. I feel out of place.

'Ah, there you are!' says Georgina, like she knew I'd come.

She points to one of the chairs and I sit down between a smartly-dressed housewife and a stout lady.

There's a buzz of excited chatter, which fades when Georgina stands up, claps her hands to get our attention and introduces herself as Miss Lloyd. I can't help noticing: *Miss*. I look down at her left hand: no ring. Lost her fiancé in the war?

Georgina tells us about the pursuit of art through the written word, about self-expression, about the creative endeavour... She stands tall, moves her hands expressively, smiles a lot. I'm drawn to her confidence and clarity, which I can't help comparing to my wife's vagueness. I think about the two sheets of paper, folded in my jacket pocket: hopeless attempts to capture the vastness of the sea and shore, written with all the clumsy seriousness of a pretentious sixth-former. Will Georgina ask me to read them? Would I dare to?

Georgina looks at her watch. 'My goodness, I've been talking far too long.'

People politely shake their heads.

'We must move on to the important part of the evening: to your work.'

A ripple of excitement runs through the room. Each of us thinks: *me! Me!*

Georgina asks us to introduce ourselves and responds to each person with a comment or question.

'How long have you been writing poetry, Mrs Sanderson?... No, rhyme isn't seen as essential anymore... Yes, Hardy's vision was *so true...*'

She has the knack of putting people at ease, and I think: I could join this group, I could attend every evening, I'd no longer be alone.

Before I know it, she turns to me.

'I'm Edmund Jenkins. I'm interested in – interested in writing nature poetry.' Is that really a form of poetry? Or have I just made it up?

'Oh, how wonderful!' says Georgina and I feel so grateful to her.

She talks to one more stout lady and the thin youth who's trying to look like a poet, then claps her hands to get our attention.

'Right, we must get to work. But first: are there any questions?'

'Miss Lloyd?'

It's one of the stout ladies. Georgina smiles at her.

'I was thinking, Miss Lloyd, about the current – the current crisis.' The lady nods towards the poster on the noticeboard. 'Would you agree that the best art always rises above politics?'

Georgina gives a little start of surprise.

'Politics?' she replies. 'Of course, the greatest writers and artists have always responded to the world around them. Think of Wilfred Owen: would he have written a word without the tragedy of the trenches?'

People round the room nod.

'And today?' the stout lady continues. 'As artists, we must try to reconcile the opposing parties, mustn't we?' Georgina looks thoughtful. 'Bring peace to the conflict?'

The stout lady smiles in a winsome, schoolgirl way that doesn't suit her.

Georgina speaks slowly. 'Of course, peace is vital.' Heads nod again. 'But there are other concerns. As a nation, we have duties, we are the world's conscience, its moral leader. We brought civilisation to half the world.'

A few nod, but most look up, wondering what she'll say next. Georgina glances round, perhaps sensing that the class isn't quite in agreement.

'We must remain true to our values, we must act decisively.'

'But—' the stout lady isn't convinced. 'Do we want another conflict? At this time? So soon after—'

'We cannot allow this Hitler on the Nile to dictate to us.' Georgina's voice has changed, her smile has disappeared. She jabs the air with her finger, pointing at the stout lady who looks surprised. 'Look at those people! Savages! Incapable of anything constructive. How could they run the Suez Canal?'

I'm on my feet. How did that happen? Everyone in the room stares at me. I'll have to say something.

There's silence. Georgina frowns, her hand falls.

Words come to my mouth from somewhere. 'My wife is one of those savages.' Anger thickens my voice. How dare this woman talk of her like that!

'Your—wife?' stutters Georgina.

'Yes, my wife.'

I walk to the door, weaving my way through the chairs, taking care not to bump into anyone. When I reach the door, I stop, turn round.

'People like you always forget that *they* built the Canal. It's *their* land.'

The class stare at me. Then the stout lady who asked the question reaches for her handbag, stands up and follows me out. I hold the door open for her.

'Honestly!' She looks at me. 'Do we really want another war? Out there in the sand.' She shakes her head. 'For what?'

I breathe deeply, try to stop my arm trembling.

'One war was enough for me,' I say. 'And they're not bad people, you know, the Egyptians.'

'Of course not! They're just like us.'

No, I think. They're not just like you. They're—they're… I think of my wife's brown eyes, of her nervousness, her moods.

I walk to the cottage. I'll pack my suitcase tonight, catch the first train to London tomorrow. I must go back to my wife. Nafah needs me.

Taff Dreaming

Denise Dyer

The prow nuzzles the water causing ripples
I lay back on the comfortable cushions and watch as clouds
float through the sky

The delicate lapping of water on wood, gently rocks my boat
shaped cot

We pass under trees reaching out their branches like fingers
trying to touch the sky

I hear the call of the kingfisher and see its flash of blue
the only thing in a hurry today

I watch the heron as it stands like a feathered ornament
a reminder that everything is worth the wait

The fluffy coot babies that only a mother can love
walk along a fallen branch
their reflections blur like an artist's palette as the silent
ripples touch them

I watch the changing reflections in the water
a pallet of mottled greens and browns with hints of blue and
sometimes inky black

I languidly touch them with my fingers
the water is cold but welcoming

A gentle breeze makes the leaves dance
I close my eyes to indulge in the scents surrounding me

With the warmth of the sun on my skin
I forget all those things I was supposed to remember not to
forget

As I drift into slumber

Chasing Shadows

Peter Gaskell

Tyres screeching out onto the main road, they sped off in the direction of Mitchelhampton. As she revved her car, Mags gave me a tissue to wipe my eyes.

'Trust me, Anne. I won't let him get away.'

Since Paul wouldn't agree to Dad coming to live with us after his operation, I'd been anxious and moody. Dad on his own was a risk to himself. Paul's insistence that the district nurse would be routinely monitoring Dad didn't convince me. Though he told me he didn't, it irked me that Paul kept his phone switched off all day.

Mags understood. So when she offered to take me out to lunch at the Cat & Mouse, I welcomed such comforting distraction.

But there outside the pub was our car, with Paul at the wheel, his mobile phone stuck to his ear and a young woman in the passenger seat. From his quick glance around as he gunned the engine, I felt sure he had seen me. They were quickly off, then us in hot pursuit. It was hard to stay in sight of them as Paul swerved around any car doing less than the speed limit, even on bends. Was he over the alcohol limit too? Then without indicating, he pulled off onto a narrow country road.

'Slow down, Mags, please,' I implored, lurching across the seat as she skidded round bends to be sure of keeping Paul in view. He must've surely known he was being tailed. My shock at our continuing speed wasn't relieved by my admiration of Mags's driving skills. Then as we were about to take a sharp corner, my ears and stomach were assaulted by a bang of crunching metal and glass.

Paul had hit a tractor. I rushed over to open the door as Mags dialed 999. Blood was running from the blonde head of Paul's unconscious passenger, darkening the pale blue of her uniform. Looking at me with incredulity and horror, groaning with pain, Paul was first to find his voice.

'I'll stay with her till the ambulance arrives. Mags, you take Anne to her father's at once. He's fallen down the stairs.'

I gasped. 'But you and the nurse... at the pub?' was all I could stammer.

'She lives next door to the pub and rang me after getting a call from Dad. We both tried ringing you.'

He groaned again. 'You really must get a new phone, Anne.'

Perceptual Surprises

Sarah Mayo

In the time it takes
your eyes
to travel
the length
of a butterfly's wingspan,

in the curve
and burst
of candy bright
dahlias regrowing,

decades leap
in a whoosh
of high-speed travel
to living

long past
a childish prediction
of death
to a future
which now says

yes.

The Other Side

Angela Edwards

The disappearance of Doris Barton led to an intensive local search, and an ever widening national one. She was 85 years old and of much decreased mobility and yet, while her younger sister Mabel was in the kitchen washing up on Christmas morning, she vanished. No progress was made in solving the mystery with very few responses to a televised reconstruction of a look-a-like Doris Barton wandering around her home in Station Road.

There were local theories. One was that she had left the house in a state of confusion and collapsed and died somewhere. But there was scepticism at the idea of an elephants' graveyard for old ladies to which they staggered off and died when the time came. More popular was the notion that she had been murdered by her younger sister who removed the body from the house on Christmas evening while the neighbours were entertaining themselves with the annual repetition of disaster films, board games, and alcohol.

The 1970 Social Services Act having amalgamated the previous departments of Child Care, Welfare and Mental Health, the case arrived on the desk of Area Head Avril Harper, formally of the Children's Department – concern now being felt for the wellbeing of the younger sister Mabel Barton, who possibly needed support. Avril passed the file on to the team that covered Mabel's address. Team Leader Jenny Matthews considered staff resources and allocated the case to Lewis Price, formally of the Mental Health Department, whom she rather distrusted on the grounds that his hands-off, liberal approach might at some point create a scandal. He was young, not long out of university, long haired, with John Lennon glasses and jeans which he saw no reason to exchange for a suit. She preferred giving him elderly clients whose collapse into mental incapacity or death would be unlikely to lead to a public enquiry.

Lewis discussed the matter with Rachel, formally of the Welfare department, and a major source of local information.

'Known as Batty Barton,' she told him. 'My grandmother was roughly the same age and knew a lot about the family.'

Lewis sat down on a desk near her. 'Anything useful?'

'The parents moved into the house when mother, Mrs Barton, was a bride and Station Road was Cherry Orchard Lane. Her husband was said to be a quiet little man in banking and Mrs Barton was the daughter of a colonel in the Indian army, she had an uncle who was General Sir somebody. She was an appalling snob, dominated the whole family and frightened the neighbours. There is a story that, when Mabel was eighteen, she fell in love with a young man who was a chemist but Mrs Barton put a stop to it because her daughter couldn't possibly marry a tradesman. Mabel was sent to the south coast to stay with an aunt for a while. My grandmother saw the young couple sobbing in each other's arms in the lane behind the chemist's shop before Mabel left. After that the two girls lived at home with their parents. They weren't allowed to work because Mrs Barton considered that nice ladies didn't. Doris Barton was very like the mother – so much so my mother says that there almost wasn't a Doris. She hadn't approved of Mabel's affair and didn't support her. Mabel was said to be quite pretty as a girl but became plain. Now she pads around town looking odd, children call her a witch and shout rude comments after her.'

Lewis knocked at the heavy door that still had its Victorian stained glass intact. He had gone up three stone steps, and went down two again when it opened, his childhood terror of the witch in Snow White kicking in. The woman who came out of a dim interior wore a bowler hat, a darned cardigan and a piece of black cloth in lieu of a skirt pinned round her waist. She looked out from dark protruding eyes on either side of a hooked nose.

'Good afternoon.' He held out his identity card. 'I'm Lewis Price from Social Services.'

She seemed impressed and the voice was deep and cultured. 'Mr Price, do come in.'

The door closed and he stepped into a different time zone. Nothing appeared to have happened here since the first world war at least. If cars had existed then they were open-topped with brass fittings. The carpets were red Axminster and furniture was ornate carved wood with a preponderance of elephants and foliage. Japanese jars shone from corners and a glass dome stood over wax grapes and artificial flowers. He followed along a dark hall under the heads of snarling animals.

'Do sit down!' she said when they reached an equally oppressive sitting room. 'And would you like some tea?'

She returned to the gloom and he looked round, noticing in particular a large gold frame enclosing a small dark print. Lifting his glasses he recognised it as the Pre-Raphaelite version of the Lady of Shallot setting out in her boat for Camelot. Mabel returned with a tray of beautiful cups and followed the direction of his eyes.

'Such a strange story!' she said. 'Mother loved Lord Tennyson's poetry, but I never could quite understand why the

Lady of Shalott died just because she looked out of the window at Sir Lancelot and then took a boat down the river.'

Lewis thought back to English lessons. 'Is it the poem where the lady is doomed to stay in the tower weaving and watching the world in her mirror, and if she looks out of the window she dies?'

'Yes, and she says, "I'm half sick of shadows". Such a sad comment!'

She went out again, walking stiffly in a pair of flat, decaying slippers, and returned with an exquisite silver teapot. He wondered why she was entertaining him and tapped the edge of his identity card on the arm of a chair as he thought.

'So very nice,' said Mabel, 'to see a proper visiting card. People used to keep them in beautiful carved cases and gave one to the maid at the door, and the maid would bring it to Mother on a tray!'

He gathered she had no idea who he was apart from someone with a proper visiting card. She poured the tea.

'We were wondering,' he said, lowering his cup to its saucer, 'if you needed any help, after the sad loss of your sister?'

'Oh, how very kind! Poor Doris! But you know it's such a strange thing. She never did want a tombstone. She used to say to me, "Mabel don't put one of those great things on top of me, I won't be able to breathe".'

Lewis retreated to casework techniques. 'It must be difficult for you!'

'Yes, I do miss her. We used to sit together at the front window for tea and I remember saying to her one day that if a nuclear bomb was dropped on London we'd have a very good view!'

Lewis glanced through the window at the distant haze that

was London and, making a brief calculation, decided that this was an optimistic view of their occupation in that event.

'And I said I wondered what would happen to all the beautiful china in the museums – the Worcester and the Crown Derby?'

He searched for an opening and decided to deal directly with the matter in hand. Anyone who was prepared to watch a nuclear explosion over the breakfast table and be primarily concerned about the fate of the china was tough.

'Have you any idea what happened to your sister?'

She hesitated. 'It is very awkward. I didn't like to say anything to the policemen because Mother was unhappy about official gentlemen coming to the house. The maid set fire to the chimney once and the fire engine came. Mother said she couldn't hold up her head in front of the neighbours for months. She was so embarrassed.'

Lewis drank his tea and waited.

'It was last autumn,' she went on. 'I was in the garden picking Michaelmas daisies. Mother always loved them, so I put them in a vase and brought them in here, where Doris could see them. She wasn't in the room. I looked round, and then I saw her. She was on the other side of the mirror! Of course, I was concerned, and I banged on the glass and said, "Doris, what are you doing in there?" but she ignored me. I was quite cross and went out to the kitchen to make tea. Then when I came back she was in her chair as usual.'

Lewis noted the big armchair on one side of the fireplace, dented with the impression of someone having sat in it for a long time.

'And after that she often did it.'

'Did she explain why?'

'We never mentioned it. Not until Christmas Eve when I

said to her, "Doris, I hope you're not going into the mirror during Christmas". I felt we ought to spend the festive season together. But she didn't say anything. Then on Christmas morning, after I had washed up the breakfast china, I came back in here and she was gone. I saw her sitting in there quite comfortably and I banged on the glass and called to her. But she ignored me.' The old mouth trembled. 'I know I shouldn't say this but Doris could be unkind. I picked up the big poker and hit the mirror with it, and I went on until it broke.'

'You broke the mirror?'

'So Doris was left on the other side. Would you like another cup of tea?'

Lewis noticed a large oblong of cleaner wallpaper to one side of the fireplace, evidently caused by a substantial object once hanging there.

'No thank you.'

At this point his team leader would recommend that he call a doctor to make an order under the Mental Health Act. He considered it. The most likely explanation was that Mabel had beaten her sister to death with a poker. One or two blows would be enough for a frail old head, and Mabel, who did all the housework and shopping, would be strong enough. He thought of two little girls playing in the old house, of corners and secret places in garden, cellar and attic where things could be hidden. And one of them was bitterly angry, having glimpsed Sir Lancelot from the window of the castle in which she was trapped, and had spent the remainder of her life weaving shadows from polite conversation and domestic concerns, and dying in her own way.

Mabel carried the tray out. There were photographs on the mantelpiece and he stood up to reach one. Two young women looked out from the silver frame, heads leaning together, one with a round face, straight dark hair, and big dark eyes, the other with a narrower face, fair hair and light eyes.

She returned and they talked about her grandfather's career in India and of the uncle who was a general. He thought of the options. There was no physical need for her to be moved out of her world, and it would almost certainly be impossible for her to adjust to another. The police had not found a body, and it wasn't his business to investigate a crime. He waited for a break in the general's story and got up.

'I'll leave my card and you must contact me if there's anything you need. And I think you shouldn't mention what happened to your sister. People might not understand!'

'Oh no!' she said, leading him out of the room. 'It would be worse than the fire engine!'

They passed an ornate waste bin and, catching a glimmer of light from it, he bent down and picked out a small piece of heavy glass. One ferocious blue eye glared back from it.

The Candle

Jade Bangs

The wispy fire atop the candle is painfully close to blowing out. Each gust of wind like a wave, nearly extinguishing the candle before a spark of hope is restored, and the flame grows bright before the next gust of wind, unexpected and dangerously stronger than the last.

If so inclined, they can protect this small candle sitting unsteadily on the mantelpiece. Closing the window would stop the faltering, the consistent hope and hopelessness, the threat of not making it the next time the gust of wind approaches. The little black latch squeaks against the onslaught and the window almost slams itself shut before the wind dies down again, giving the candle a single moment to breathe.

Barely seconds pass before the next gust comes, a cold edge accompanying it this time that is almost enough to snuff out the sad little candle. The screaming of the latch continues, the shrill nearly drowned out by the roar. Once again, the window nearly slams shut, the small length of metal holding on desperately. The flame falters and for a moment it isn't sure if it can regain its strength, but the gust settles, and the flame returns.

Too strong a wind, and the candle will blow out, but it will close the window. So, the flame's hope returns just like every other time, prepared to face the wind that will inevitably come. The latch squeaks and the breeze comes with full force, bringing all it has in this personal war against the candle. And once again, like every other time, the candle nearly dies, and the wind can see its victory coming close. But the metal's whimpering has turned to a brittle shrieking alongside the fickle latch, and whilst the wind tries its hardest to blow out the candle, it also manages to slam the window shut, the metal sighing as it slots into its perfect position.

The candle's wick is unsure. The wind has left, save for a gentle breeze that enters the gaps of the window where the latch is no longer secure. But this breeze is different from the wind, as its gentle meandering through the room is enough to feed the candle without threatening it. The window whistles with the breeze and a small orange spark returns, slowly growing higher, unwilling to become a flame until it is sure. The whistling encourages the flame, an echo of the wind it used to be.

With every blow of the breeze, the flame regains its strength and its composure, finally able to secure its place atop that mantelpiece, aided only by the ghost of what the wind used to be.

The orange light glows, proud of its achievement, proud of its position and its strength to withstand the wind, unaware of how the wax melts away beneath it, slowly snaking its way in white trails down the mantelpiece, threatening the life of the flame with more savagery than the wind ever could.

Cardiff

Jeff Robson

Dank and dismal she was unloved
As written by the sages
A capital city born of work
Black with the dust of ages
Steel and coal her life blood
So many workers gave so much
To earn their daily bread
Then coal was lost, steel production ceased
The new bay became a playground
That changed an ugly beast
Nowadays the air is clean
The bay is full of boats
Dirt and grime is never seen
Upon the buildings floats
Cardiff lives again different than before
A nicer place to live
Of this we can be sure

Guilty

Paul Jauregui

'Where are the bodies?'

'I didn't kill them.'

'So where are your wife and children?'

A shrug.

'Explain the hospital visits. Your searches about hiding money and body disposal. Your secret lover.'

Whispered: 'I've done nothing.'

'They're dead, aren't they?'

***

Hidden from view she watches, as he's taken away.

It had been difficult; using his laptop, diverting money, inventing the girlfriend.

But it worked.

They were free.

No more screaming.

No more violence.

Just freedom.

Spag Bol

Ian McNaughton

The game was up, Mum caught me on the chair trying to knock off the strands of spaghetti stuck to the ceiling.

'One, two, three, four, five, six, seven, eight, nine, ten,' she calmly counted and gave me a beaming false smile. She wasn't counting the spaghetti that's for sure as there had to be at least twenty still dangling up there.

The cookbook said that you can tell when the pasta is cooked as it will not stick to the ceiling. Mum pointed out that I had misread it.

It had been a few days since I had been locked in the pantry for misbehaving. I had also been banned from the kitchen for the chip pan thing, or 'fire', as Mum liked to call it. She said she didn't mind me cooking where there weren't flames involved. I asked if lollypops were OK, and she said they were… she didn't get my sarcasm. She had been in an oddly good mood since she started doing the counting to ten thing, which she did quite often with deep breathing.

I kept telling her that I wasn't going to be a world-famous chef if I wasn't allowed in the kitchen.

She said I wasn't going to be anything if I caused any more fires.

'Sally James's mother lets her cook,' I complained.

'Well, go over there and burn their house down then.'

So, I did.

Mrs James was told off by the firemen for allowing young children to have access to cookers without supervision.

Sally and I had made a Victoria sponge cake and went out to play for thirty minutes at gas mark four while it baked. Her neighbour spotted the smoke and called the fire brigade.

We arrived back just as Sally's mum was getting home from work.

'I told you we should have taken the clock,' said Sally. I said I was convinced we hadn't been gone that long and prided myself with a good sense of food timing. I didn't understand.

We strolled innocently into the house.

A firefighter was cupping what looked like the burnt shards of an oven glove. Sally's face turned as red as the fire engine. We slipped back out.

The only real damage was the smell of smoke and my credibility.

The whole street of Heol Chapel had been relatively quiet throughout the event. It was only when my mother turned up did curtains start to twitch and doors open, and a crowd gathered outside Sally's house. The rumour of how Mum went berserk when I did anything wrong had until then been just that. No one had witnessed the volcano erupt but just heard that when it blew it was an awesome sight. Tremors could be felt from my house when I was in trouble, but until now, it had been from behind closed doors.

'Again, I'm ever so sorry, Doris, be sure I'm going to punish him when I get him home.'

'It's fine, Pat,' Sally's mum replied. 'Don't be too hard on the boy, as I said, it's more Sally's fault. Her dad is going to go ballistic when he gets in.'

Like a leopard, Mum slunk up the garden path looking for

her prey amongst the crowd. She spotted me and was off the blocks like Colin Jackson in a 110m hurdle final.

I don't know why I ran; with each stride, I could see a day being added to my incarceration. In no time at all the cheers from the neighbours were a distant mumble, I looked around to see Mum leaning against a lamppost catching her breath, waving an angry fist.

This wasn't going to end well.

I dawdled to Whitchurch Park, kicked up leaves and sat on a swing. It started to rain, and I was wearing a T-shirt. Why on earth did I run? I could be home now in a dry pantry reading something warming like shepherd's pie.

The wind was cold, and I was wet, I should go home and face the music. This was surely up there with the whisky thing a few weeks ago. I was locked away for hours, it would have been overnight had Dad not woken at two a.m. saying to Mum that he couldn't remember seeing me go to bed. I couldn't remember much of the whole whisky thing apart from me never wanting to have any alcohol for the rest of my life and Mum shaking me awake on the pantry floor and sending me up to my room.

I was just about to go home when through the slapping of the rain on the leaves and cranking branches, I heard a meow. I looked up and in the tree above me, I saw a ginger cat.

I tried coaxing it down with an array of cat calling sounds. It just cried louder. I could get up, but it would be a difficult climb.

There wasn't anyone else around to ask for help and I sure wasn't going to call the fire brigade.

On my third fall, I landed on the same part of my backside as I had after the first. I was sore, wet and hungry.

I decided to try once more before calling it a day and leaving the cat to fall on its arse instead; it was bound to find a way down when it needed food. I took a run-up, bounced off the trunk and grabbed a branch. Not knowing what my next move was going to be, I hung in limbo staring up at the cat who stared back. It stopped meowing. I think he was enjoying the entertainment. I swung my legs up and latched them around the same branch then let go with my hands, I was now in the exact same spot but upside down. Before all the blood in my body found its way to my head, I heaved myself up so that all my limbs and head were reunited in a horizontal position. The branch above me was easier and within no time I was almost in reach of the cat but rather high up.

The wind was howling, and the tree was creaking. I put my hand out to coax the cat nearer when an almighty crack made it shoot off higher up the tree and made me almost shit myself.

Branch number one was gone. There was no way I was going to get down. This realisation came along with the one that if I had got the cat, how did I intend to climb down with it? Like the spaghetti, I hadn't planned things out too well. Today was not a good one. The rain turned it up a notch. To make it worse the cat clambered down and sat beside me purring and rubbing up against me.

Close by the sky was belching out cracks of thunder and an explosion of megaton webs lit up the park. The storm was upon me and I was in a tree. Was it a coincidence that our teacher talked about conductivity yesterday? I had homework on it; I'd prefer not to have hands-on experience though. I decided there and then that if I wasn't toasted by a streak of lightning, I would give up cooking and the idea of becoming a chef forever and become a fireman.

I would live next to a park with lots of trees and walk around it a lot, looking up. I'd be on the lookout for cats and small boys.

I saw someone at the far end of the park near the library walking a dog. I shouted as loud as I could. The wind and rain drowned me out. It was now getting dark and I was feeling sorry for myself. I needed a wee.

At least I wasn't going to die alone, I thought. I stroked the cat to reassure it and myself. I mean to reassure us both; I didn't stroke myself. The next clap of thunder was so loud that what was dammed up in my bladder burst down my trouser leg. Some of it blew back up, I know because it was warm. The cat clawed its way up my face and took a leap of faith off the top of my head. It looked very majestic as it glided through the sky like a pro, sprawled out in a star shape. It hit the ground on all fours, turned up to look at me and scuttled off into the bushes. My face was stinging from the scratches that were bleeding.

I wondered if I wasn't the only child he had lured up the tree.

I was going to have to climb down and jump. Broken legs would be less painful than a bolt of lightning.

Ten, nine, eight, seven, six, five, four, three…

'Lloyd!'

Someone was calling my name.

'Lloyd! Lloyd!'

Lots of people were calling my name, their torch lights were floating and bouncing around the park. I cried out but the voices kept calling.

'I'm up here, in the tree.'

'Lloyd! Lloyd!'

'I'm up here!' I screamed.

They were walking past me.

I started to cry.

'What you doing up there, Lloyd?'

'Hi, Dad,' I sobbed.

'He's over here everyone, I've found him.'

Within no time at all the beams of light shone on me like a spotlight on a stage. Normally with this amount of attention, I would have done my party trick but felt it inappropriate. I shyly waved down to what seemed like twenty people and smiled. Old lady 'Cursing Constance' shouted up that I was a fucking liability and should be left up there and asked if I'd seen her ginger cat on my travels.

Ten minutes later a familiar face greeted me up the tree.

'Hello, Lloyd, keeping us busy today, aren't you, young man,' said the fireman.

Under the supervision of my mother the following day, I cooked enough spaghetti bolognaise to feed an army.

Although it was a bit cold and the ground still soggy, neighbours brought over tables and chairs to join us in our meal to say thank you. A row of happy people stood in line with their bowls and plates, I stood behind three large pots of the sauce and dolloped it lovingly onto the pasta my father had dished out, my sister and mother sprinkled the parmesan and salad, and my brother poured the drinks.

Sally James brought over loads of cream Victoria sponge cakes. Everyone complimented me on my dish and said that I should become a chef. I silently agreed with them but vowed to keep looking up trees whenever I went through a park on the way to my restaurant.

Rexit

Stephen Pritchard

'Your Majesty, make this the year we cast off our European shackles. God had a purpose in creating our country an island.'

'Continue, Archbishop. We like what we are hearing.'

'His purpose is that, from the security of our borders, we go forth, to become the greatest power the world has ever known. And a benefactor to less fortunate nations.'

'We are tempted, Archbishop.'

'Majesty, Harold, if I may, 1066 can truly be your year.'

Flight

Sarah Mayo

An eye rises
winged by its lashes
iris imbued
with the iridescence
of a sky jeweled
an essence
caressed
by empyreal air

a release
from the tick tock
fall
of time and space

A Lesson from Celia

Nick Dunn

I would that every word I spoke
served to lift you up to Heaven,
to take your place among the stars.

You are clearly of their number:
they glitter in your eyes,
they sparkle in your smile.

Alas!
My words are clumsy,
clunky,
ill-formed lumps of clay,
feet on which no pedestal
should stand.

Perhaps I should not raise you so.
For you are merely human,
one who snores,
one who farts,
one who snorts
when they laugh.

But so do I,
and that makes all the difference.

Men for the Job

Martin Buckridge

We witness a sharp crack of heads by the courthouse coffee shop as two strangers simultaneously bend forward to place their bags on the floor. Heads spinning, John the barista and Mr John the barrister remember their names but not their respective professions. Each staggers away with the other's bag.

Each is approached by a busy woman looking for a man called John. Mr John is led to a changing area in the coffee shop and John to the court robing room.

'This is going to be fun,' thinks John as he takes the horsehair wig and black robe from his bag and tries them on in front of the mirror.

Mr John pulls from his bag an apron with the vaguely familiar word *barista* printed on the bib. He puzzles at the gleaming coffee machine and thinks, 'It's strange I don't remember how it works. I wonder if they've got a kettle.' After studying the long and confusing coffee menu Mr John watches his new colleague make an Americano. 'That doesn't look too difficult,' he thinks before deciding to keep it simple by persuading each customer they only want an Americano.

To John's left stands the defendant, the jury to his right, a bored looking judge faces him. John tries to recall what people are supposed to say in situations like this, but all that comes to mind are court scenes from *Law and Order* and *Judge Rinder*. In a flash of desperation John turns to the defendant and booms,

'Why don't you just plead guilty? We all know you are we can see it in your face.'

'I thought you were defending this man,' interrupts the judge.

John's heart misses a beat but he recovers quickly. 'Ahhh. Just checking you were still awake, my lord. I must say, you're looking a little sleepy. Would you like me to make you a nice strong coffee? Triple shot?'

Mr John gives his first customer a long stare of the sort designed to cast doubt in the recipient. 'Madam. What was your state of mind when you requested a Cappuccino? Let me direct your attention to this Americano. I put it to you this is what you really wanted... no madam, you cannot approach. You have exhausted the subject; please move on.'

The day is long for our two heroes, even longer for those they encounter. As the sun sets over the courthouse they meet again. 'What a terrible day,' moans Mr John. 'My customers were ungrateful; they called me a despot and refused to drink my coffee.'

'That's nothing,' responds John. 'The judge shouted at me, the jury laughed and the man I was defending wept.'

Each walks away thinking, 'Phew. I'm glad I don't have his job. Now, where do I live?'

Terrible Weather for June

Jennifer Wilkinson

JUNE

'Terrible weather for June,' he said, shuffling his feet and glancing at the girl, then back at his feet.

'June who?' she asked.

'June, the month June,' he replied.

'Oh, yes, of course. How silly of me!' They stood in the drizzle for a moment, then she said, 'My mother's roses have been completely drenched.'

'How awful,' he replied, but he didn't know much about roses so he said nothing else.

The sky drizzled down on them and the cars splashed past. The bus came and they both got on and went to work.

JULY

'Dreadful business about the rainforests,' she said, hoping he'd heard about the rainforests.

'The rainforests? Oh yes – dreadful. A terrible state of affairs,' he said, tucking his book about roses under his arm. 'Most disturbing. Would you like an Extra Strong Mint?'

'Thank you.'

They sucked their Extra Strong Mints and a breeze blew across them. The bus came and they both got on and went to work.

AUGUST

'Are you going on holiday soon?' he asked.

'Yes, I'm going to Blackpool – in a week, for a fortnight,' she smiled. 'And you?

'I'm going to Skegness – in a fortnight, for a week.'

'How nice.' They both laughed. 'I hope the weather's good for you – Skegness can be *so* bracing.'

'Yes, that's what the brochure said.'

They both laughed again. The sun shone down on them and the cars whizzed past. The bus came and they both got on and went to work.

SEPTEMBER

'Did you have a nice holiday?' she enquired.

'Very nice, thank you. Very relaxing. And you?'

'Oh, lovely, thank you. Lovely weather.'

'The weather makes all the difference, I always think.'

'Oh, I think so too. All the difference.'

They both watched the clouds as the clouds floated past. Then the bus came and they both got on and went to work.

OCTOBER

'Awful shame the leaves are dying,' he remarked.

'Yes, awful shame. They do look so pretty while they fall though.'

'True, they are pretty. And there'll be more next year.'

'Yes. I like the spring. I like the autumn too, though.'

'Yes, I like autumn. But I like spring best.'

'Oh, I agree.'

They watched the birds gather on the wires, ready to leave. Then the bus came and they both got on and went to work.

NOVEMBER
In November a temporary secretary caught their bus for a month, so nobody said anything.

DECEMBER
'Have you done your Christmas shopping yet?' she asked.
    'Oh yes, weeks ago. Have you?'
    'No, not yet.'
    The rain came down and ruined his hair and her make up. Then the bus came and they both got on and went to work.

JANUARY
'Did you have a merry Christmas?' he enquired.
    'Very merry, thank you.'
    'And a happy New Year?'
    'Yes, very happy. Did you make any resolutions?'
    'Only one.'
    'I made one too.'
    She wondered if she should ask him what his resolution was or if that would be prying. Then the bus came and they both got on and went to work.

FEBRUARY
'I do think the snow's pretty,' she told him.
    'Terribly cold though.'
    'Oh, very cold. My mother suffers dreadfully from the cold, in her legs.'
    'In her legs?'
    'Yes, her legs.'
    'I'm sorry to hear that.'
    They watched the snow fall and shivered. Then the bus came and they both got on and went to work.

MARCH

'Terribly windy,' he panted, after running to retrieve his hat.

'Dreadfully windy,' she agreed, turning her umbrella the right way round.

'Does your mother suffer from this?'

'From wind? No, our house is very secure against wind.'

'That's good.'

'Yes.'

He clung to his hat and she hung on to her umbrella. Then the bus came and they both got on and went to work.

APRIL

'Are you celebrating St George's Day?' she asked.

'No, I didn't think you could.'

'Well, I don't think anyone does, but I don't see why not.'

'No, it's a good idea. We'll have to remember it next year. Have to have a party.'

'Have a party! Any excuse!'

He thought about a party and calculated how much it would cost. Then the bus came and they both got on and went to work.

MAY

'Lovely weather,' he observed.

'Yes, lovely for a wedding.'

'Are you getting married?' he asked, surprised.

'No, but my cousin is. She's a year younger than me.'

'I love a wedding.'

'Yes, they're lovely. I'll be three times the bridesmaid.'

He wondered if that was good as they watched the birds flying to and fro and the cars speeding past them. Then the bus came and they both got on and went to work.

JUNE

'Terrible weather for June,' he said, standing in the rain.

'Yes, it is, and I think I need a change.'

She crossed the road and walked away from the bus stop. When the bus came only he got on and went to work.

A Witness

Sarah Mayo

A goldfinch flits
from the seeker's view.
A split-second colour flash
in a fragment
of loaded conversation
the crux unsaid.

A slurring sway of swiggers
stumble
on the path pounded
by runners
with intent
etched on their faces.

The yew tree vaunts
dressed in emerald plumage
as the stoic riverbank
hosts spright songbirds springing,
billowing plastic bags
lost.

Mallards glide free
from becoming
take-away meals. Herons
hide in the camera obscura

of poets' eyes, merging
with the meandering motion

Whose lungs are clear once more,
the mills and muck washed
from her flowing mind. Bound
for the mouth to mother,
she sweeps past walking leaves,
mere dust blowing.

Losing my Dad

Suzanne Sheperd

I wasn't with Dad when he took his last breath; I'd only
stepped away
And I live with that guilt and emptiness every single day
Dad was my hero, my Superman, I the apple of his eye
It was hard to watch him growing old, harder watching him
die
I appreciated every moment I was blessed to have him while
a child
I supported every aspect of his life as he grew weaker, more
meek and mild
It was Dad who used to cook for me and bathe me when I
was young
How things change and roles reverse and daughter becomes
the mum
I'm glad I had the chance to do the things I did for Dad
But I do miss those things I did, and that still makes me sad.

The Sea Maiden

Ruth Hogger

She knew she was swimming closer to the surface than would have been advised by the elders who went before her. It was late to be swimming south for the winter. She could not stop to rest for long where water meets air – the blood would freeze in her veins.

But then, who was left but her to heed the neuroses of her ancestors? They were all long lost to the deep. The lucky ones were released back into the energy of the waves centuries ago, their bones ground down until they were nothing but silt in the forgotten depths. Some of her ancestors had not been granted that mercy.

Sea maidens had taken men for lovers for as long as men had dreams. Grandmother used to sing an old song that pronounced maidens and men to have similar hearts. The words as her grandmother sang them were long forgotten to her now, but she remembered the lesson. Though crews of men were cruel, many men did love; and though many maidens loved, many returned their cruelty. Miracles from the deep rescued men who surely would have drowned; and maidens stranded upon shores were returned to the safety of the waves. Maidens of the sea left their worlds behind to love men and mother their children – some by choice, others still due to the trickery and deceit of their captors. Millennia of distrust crept by, and still men gazed guilelessly across glittering oceans, oblivious to the generations of pain that broiled beneath the surface. Many's the maiden who lured a ship onto the rocks with her sweet song wailing on the winds of a storm; in their turn, men grew ever more cruel, hunting maidens under guise of sport and curiosity. Seeking sanctuary from men above the waves, maidens sought the safety of the dark in shoals. Grandmother sang that the old ones turned blind and spineless, their skin grey and slimy, and somewhere along countless cursed eons of sightless scavenging for rotten flesh, they lost all reason. Now, a maiden could swim for thousands of miles of ocean without encountering another of her kind. Perhaps she never would again.

Opposing the cautionary tales of the old ones, the sea maiden surfaced to examine her skin under the sun. Clear as glass, it lay bare tributaries of green and purple veins, betraying her vulnerability. Though the days were brief, they would lengthen the further south she travelled – she must take care.

Many lifetimes ago when she was a young maid of the sea, she was curious. Her grandmother warned her to stay in the dark, and not to swim too close to the sun. But the few glimmering shafts of light that penetrated the depths were so magical – they danced a silent melody that was mysterious to her yet seemed somehow familiar. When she confided in her grandmother how she longed for the light, her grandmother beat her with love and fear in her heart, with hope that her precious granddaughter might never long for the light again.

Time passed by with no mark of night or day in the unchanging depths, until there came a time when Grandmother went to sleep and would not wake up. And so, with nothing else to turn to, the young sea maiden swam towards the only thing of any difference in her world.

Now, as she dived beneath the surface, she remembered her first journey towards the sun centuries ago. She remembered watching with wonder as light crept into her world of shadows. When she broke the surface it shattered into a million sparkling shards – she had never felt such joy before or since. She had never felt anything like the radiance of the sun. It so entranced her, she spent hours paddling on her back in its warming rays, until it burnt lesions into her skin that stung in the salty seawater.

She longed for the taste of brine in her feathered gills as she descended now. In the open ocean she could sink three hundred fathoms deep and ease the aching chill in her bones, taste the heaviness of the water in her lungs. But the waterways through which she must make her escape were bleak, bland and shallow. With the cease of endless day, ice crept across the sea with quiet determination. Winter would not sleep, and so neither could she. With little time to rest or hunt, she had grown accustomed to the gnawing hunger in her belly. Now she could ignore it no longer, and so she sought out shadows for sustenance.

Spiralling down through waters that hindered sight, the sea maiden sheathed her eyes in their tough inner lids and sank into a reverie of echoes and sensation. The waters washed away all illusions of time and space, as they always did. Her mind thus obscured, when a ship emerged from the murky waters to encroach upon her inner world of whispers and ghosts, she could not discern whether it belonged to the realm of reality, phantasy, or long forgotten memory.

The sea maiden had encountered ships beneath the waves before. This one carried three masts – broken as they were, still they loomed so tall in the gloom that she could hardly see the deck from their height. She swam a sea maiden's plait between them, until curiosity tempted her from the path of her ritual. A mysterious tunnel rising from the deck echoed to her like a siren's song. She answered its call. Gripping its rim, it was colder upon her skin than biting polar winds. Peering tentatively over the edge, she found herself exposed to a void that sent shivers crackling down her spine and through her flesh.

She told herself that the violent shake of her head was a shiver, and turned her back upon it. Abandoning the deck she swam from stern to bow, dragging her hand across the language of men and counting no less than three hundred handspans along the hull. For the last sixty counted, the ship was plated with scales as cold as the rim of the void, and a further sixty handspans took the measure of a great spar jutting from the prow. The sea maiden had never encountered a ship of this size, but she had a sense of something stranger still that slipped just beyond her grasp – something unnerving, writhing restlessly in some hidden corner of her unconscious.

She followed the prow of the ship downwards and reached understanding where the cold scales vanished into silt. She swam back along the length of the ship to be certain... around the towering rudder at the stern... and along the far side...

All ships she had ever found sleeping beneath the seas had fallen to their sides. This vessel rested proud upon its bed. The sea maiden could hear the old tales so clearly now, she could almost feel her grandmother's wrinkled lips pressed close to her ear as they whispered tragic tales of sunken ships and souls, cursed to drift beneath the waves for all eternity.

The sea maiden stared at the deck, far above. She could turn her tail, press on with her journey, push it under the surface of her mind... But her stomach gaped wide as the darkness of the void, and she was desperate enough to know that the rations of a sunken ship were too precious to leave to rot. Still, apprehension weighed heavily upon her as she began her ascent, and only the hope of scavenging strange, salted flesh gave her strength to go on.

Rising to the deck, she found a large bell lying upon its side, cankered with rust and algal gangrene. Her grandmother's sorrowful singing echoed in her memory:

There was an old helmsman who forsook his wife
And children to follow the sea,
I sang him a song and he swore on his life He would die before parting
    with me.
A more beautiful voice he never did hear
And he begged and he pleaded he might Forevermore sleep with my
    song in his ear
As he steered through the darkness of night.

As bell is to the soul of ship, so heart is to the maiden's soul.
Turn the glass and strike the bell; let it knell and let it toll.
Turn the glass and sound eight bells, and steer the ship upon the rocks.
Join me where my sisters dwell; this ship shall never reach the docks.

I loved him, by the stars above,
Believed his words were true;
But by the time I reached my love His lips were cold and blue.
So strike the bell and stab my heart
And leave me in the deep;
The sea has torn our souls apart And left me here to weep.

· Swimming closer she could see inside the bell's husk; its bloom of red rashes, mottled greens and gruesome purple. It had become a vessel for creatures of many eyes and many legs that scuttled and stared, unblinking.

Peeling her eyes and body away, she searched the midships for an open hatch. Hatch after hatch was closed to her. When she eventually found an opening, there was only just enough room for her body to slither by. The tunnel of the hatch was rimed with slimy seaweed, and her scales shivered a wave as she passed through its wet kiss, down into the belly of the wreck. Though her eyes were large pearlescent orbs evolved through millennia in the gloom, countless pounding heartbeats passed before they adjusted to the darkness.

The hatch opened into a larger space. Eyes focusing, she saw that a table lay on its side in one corner, and from another a wooden chest materialised. Her heart skipped a beat. But inside she found no more than two glass bottles and a cold, rusted container. The sea maiden wore her flowing hair with two fine fishtail plaits radiating from each temple, and now she unfastened the cruelly barbed fisherman's hook that bound them, so that the current sighing through the ship unravelled her plaits as a playful sister might.

She stabbed with the hook, piercing through rust to the flesh inside. The smell seeped all around her, and it was more instinct than pleasure that drove her to guzzle the contents in three swift slurps. It did little to fill the gaping void of her stomach.

A doorway materialised at the edge of her field of vision. The prospect of further findings was a tempting lure, but on the other hand, she might search the whole wreck and find nothing. She could not afford to lose herself in a dark labyrinth with no promise of deliverance from hunger. She fled from the dark grin of the doorway and up through the hatch before she had time to change her mind.

Emerging once more, she welcomed the sight of tiny silver fish. They shone like knives, darting in and out of frilled kelp that ribboned away through the water like flowing blood. She turned to flow away too, but as she swam past the stern cabin she choked through her gills. Could that be another maiden she saw swimming in the dark?

They rushed to meet one another, halting either side of the wall. Only when outstretched fingertips kissed glass did the sea maiden know her own reflection.

With her heavy heart sinking under wave after wave of

sorrow, she dragged her hand along the stern as she swam away from this sad, lonely place; over glass, wood, glass, wood, glass, wood —

Her hand fell into a void.

The last window had lost its pane. She gazed into the darkness, and it made her head ring.

What if there *was* one of her kind to be found?

What use would it be anyway, to live on for centuries, and share life with no other?

She swam into the dark.

Until her eyes tuned in, she was blind. Gradually the shadows surrendered their intensity. Except one shadow in the corner, which remained.

As the shadow paled, every detail of its horror grew louder and louder, until its shrill piercing scream possessed her and she could not look away.

A large man sat bolt upright in a chair. These frigid waters had the peculiarity of not only halting the ravages of time upon sunken ships, but also upon the bodies of their dead. However, the most disarming sight was the cadaver's sardonic smile. As her eyes widened in terror, his grin only seemed to grow wider in turn.

Was it a trick of her imagination? She swore she saw the corpse shift in its seat.

Then it gave a lurch that could not be denied, as though it were a dead fish being dragged along by a fisherman's line. It was standing now, retching, though its eyes and face showed no signs of life. Convulsions from its stomach moved up through its torso, up through its throat, so that she could see the muscles of its neck undulating… as though the dead man were choking up a terrible secret he had harboured alone in silence for too long…

Before the petrified sea maiden's eyes, his terrible grin parted to reveal row upon row of needle-sharp teeth. With an unnatural jolt his neck snapped back on his shoulders. The monstrous teeth rose from his open mouth – but to the sea maiden's disgust there followed a long fleshy tube, as though the dead man were purging the innards from his corpse. Only when the sea maiden spied two dull pearls beneath brackish skin did she know the dead man to be no more than a shell.

The sea maiden felt disturbance in the dark waters around her. She could not see them in the gloom, but she could sense long, sinewy ribbons of muscle whipping all around her. Sensing herself entrapped within their current, she became light-headed, and struggled to draw water through her gills. She tried to move towards the window frame, but the water felt somehow denser. Time stagnated, trapped in a nightmare where she was turning to stone. And all the while, the dead man disgorged the serpentine parasite.

Tearing her eyes from them, she hurled herself towards the window, breaking through a writhing wall.

Convulsing her gills as fresh water flowed through them, she fled for the sunlight. Throwing a glance over her tail she saw the wreck spewing rivers of putrid flesh, streaming towards her like the tentacles of some monstrous abomination. She could hear their bodies whispering against each other; they were almost upon her. She quickened the quivering of her lateral fins even as her frozen muscles cramped, pushing premonitions of tangled coils and suffocating slime from her mind.

As they ascended higher the creatures began to drop away one by one, as though the shafts of light pierced through them like swords – until suddenly, the sea maiden found herself alone once more.

For You

Morgan Fackrell

I am easily distracted,
Moving pictures, sea gulls,
The breeze gently caressing soft curtains.

You are steadfast in your determination
To see justice done,
Before it is too late.

Your voice is weak,
I pretend not to strain
to hear.
I am strong by keeping a part
Of me distant, not in this room.
With its hissing pumps and smell
Of death's presence.

Your hands are frail,
And I try not to hold on
too tightly.
But, I want to hold you fast against
The rushing tide that has us
Unsteady, frightened, brave
And furious.

Smiling you pull me back to you
And tell me it will be ok.
I say nothing
Because it won't
It can't
And I will never be ok
Again.

You tell me to carry on in that
Soft lilting tone
that was a balm to my soul.
And now sets my eyes
On fire.

We have a few hours at best,
Yet the end of your journey finds you
As strong and courageous
As when I first met you
Lean limbed, sun tanned, green eyes
Burning bright.

I will be here until the room finds silence
And I will take that silence with me
To fill my emptiness.

I will do my best over time
To be ok for you
And for me

Unlocked Love

Pamela Cartlidge

Monica swore as she scrabbled on her hands and knees looking for her spare key. Locking herself out on a bitter, dark night after another unsuccessful attempt at speed dating increased her frustration. Then her mobile died leaving her without a torch. Her shrill expletives shrouded despair.

'Can I help you?'

Monica gawked at the good-looking man bending over her. The strong light of his mobile illuminated his smiling face. 'Oh yes please,' she murmured.

When the Daisies go to Sleep

Jeff Robson

I will be there for you forever
Whenever you need me my darling girl
You are the loveliest little person
I feel so privileged to be your granddad
And honoured that you hug me so tightly
As you slip into slumber's embrace
At that time of the evening
When the daisies go to sleep
You run like the wind
Through the meadow of my garden
So happy so free, laughing all the while
Such a joy to be with you my darling girl
My heart is yours, you melt it with your smile
Time when your busy day is over
Tiredness and weariness have come
Exactly at that time of the evening
When the daisies go to sleep

HUMAN_3RR0R

Paul Mackay

Jessica was asleep when her car, following a direction from its sat-nav to drive straight on, did exactly that, off a cliff-top bend.

She woke just before hitting the bottom of the ravine.

The accident made international headlines. The first fatality since driver-less cars had been sanctioned by western governments. Questions asked whether the cause had been user error, software glitch or more worryingly, a malicious hack. The insurance companies, without precedents to guide them, would be arguing liability for decades to come.

'Whatever they say, remember what we're here for. Don't let them distract you. Never forget what they did.'

Trey's face was an oasis of calm for Molly Gardiner, Jessica's mother, as the external elevator rocketed up the Ubivis building in central San Francisco, each level zipping past with a percussive *ffft* sound. She found it helped to steady herself in his warm, compassionate gaze.

'I haven't been this focused since Jessica died,' she said.

After the accident the corporate 'highers' had been quick to offer their condolences but were not so fast to admit guilt.

Once the usual external interferences of hacking and terrorism had been eliminated as the cause, the investigation turned, at Ubivis' suggestion, to user error. Data logs and telemetry were analysed. Although Jessica had been sleeping at the time of the crash – not unusual in vehicles with no physical human interfaces – the black box indicated she had not given the car any instruction to set the accident in motion.

This did not, however, stop Ubivis from running a surreptitious media campaign to focus liability on Jessica.

It was Molly's persistence and tenacity that finally uncovered the truth.

Ella Graham fiddled with the controls of her Smart-Chair. Despite her wrist-tab handshaking with it, for some reason it hadn't configured itself to her favoured seating profile. No matter, she'd get someone in facilities to take a look at it later but now she had to run through the meeting with Seth again. As head of HR it was her job to know people and she knew Seth well enough to not quite trust him with them.

'Before you say anything, remember that Mrs Gardiner is grieving. Adjust your tone. Speak softly. Be calm. Measured. Don't say anything that may upset her.'

'He's not a fucking child,' Cyrus interrupted. Seth cut him dead with a raised hand.

At eighteen years old, Seth Prendergast was one of the smartest people on the planet, and a billionaire thanks to Cyrus, who as CFO of Ubivis, had monetised his dream of connecting the graphene chips inside every piece of equipment and furniture on Earth.

'Why are they coming?' said Seth without even turning from his work. 'Didn't we give her enough money?'

'Because they want to make a difference,' Ella replied. 'Just be nice.'

'The guy – Trey – he's the one to worry about. As long as you look sad for Mrs Gardiner then she'll be no problem. But 'Users First'? No. Still not too sure about them,' Cyrus added. 'Wannabe anti-tech terrorist organisation if ever there was.'

'They're just a lobby group. Consider this a damage limitation exercise. It'll look good in the news-loops.'

She wasn't even sure if Seth was listening. Fully focused on the holographic charms that floated above his desk-top, he moved and chopped coloured blocks of code across his workspace. Seth's latest obsession. He had tunnel vision once a project interested him and he'd been working this one since the accident. As always, the rest of the board left him to do his own thing, secure in the knowledge he was creating even more income streams for them.

The elevator slowed to a stop and opened into a small antechamber that led into the top office that occupied the entirety of the Ubivis building's spire. Only a featureless gunmetal door barred entry. Trey and Molly stepped up to the door as the elevator slid back down to lower levels. There were no visible handles, buttons or levers. Whatever mechanism the door used to allow access was hidden from view.

'Are we supposed to knock?' asked Molly.

It had been a gamble on Molly's part to hire a specialist software engineer to review the car's code. It was expensive and the legal battle to get Ubivis to release their intellectual property to a third party would have bankrupted her if they hadn't identified the 'race condition' bug responsible for Jessica's death. A conspiracy of unfortunate events – a microsecond delay on a sat nav signal and a stacked road that curled its way up a steep valley slope – that led to the vehicle navigating off the ravine. Events can be anticipated and code written to deal with it, but the time allocated to beta testing was too limited to rehearse the unique combination of conditions responsible for Jessica's car crash. Not if the project was to be delivered within budget and on time.

The software coding error detected once experienced, Ubivis

paid ten million dollars to Molly to keep her findings out of the public domain. The public's trust in Ubivis and their products were worth much, much more than that minuscule overhead.

The elevator notified Ella's wrist-tab of Trey and Molly's arrival.

'They're here.'

Cyrus gestured at the smart-door. There was no response.

'Why isn't it opening?'

Cyrus and Ella stepped forward to the door. Cyrus gesturing again.

'Open sesame,' he said. The door remained closed.

Seth stepped forward and made the same gesture. There was still no response. It remained stubbornly inanimate.

On the other side, Molly and Trey waited. They knocked but the door was heavily insulated. A holographic image appeared alongside them of Cyrus, with Seth and Ella behind him.

'Hello. I'm Cyrus Holland, CFO of Ubivis. We've got a problem with the smart-door. It's not responding to our commands so I'm afraid we're unable to let you in right now.'

Trey rolled his eyes at Molly.

'This is exactly what Users First campaigns against,' he said to her, then turning to the image: 'Perhaps you should consider putting a handle on a door. Or some kind of manual override even.'

'Sure. Why not go back to the dark ages?' Seth said. 'Humans cause more prob—' Ella pushed her way into view.

'Hi. We're working on getting the door open. So looking forward to finally meeting with you.'

The hologram snapped off.

Ella watched as Seth opened the door's command protocols on his desktop.

'Reception transmitted their biometrics to the door so they should have access.'

The door flashed red briefly, a lock clicked, then turned back to its gunmetal hue.

'That shouldn't have happened,' said Seth.

Molly and Trey had seen the flash of light. The hologram reappeared with Ella at the forefront.

'Hi. Er... I don't want you to panic – it's really, really important that you don't – but we have a slight issue with the door.'

'But you're getting it fixed are you not? How long will this take?' Trey asked.

'You both need to relax. Maybe sit down. Take short shallow breaths.'

'What?' asked Molly.

'Calm please. We will get you out but –' Ella took a deep breath herself.

'The door has entered lock-down mode. We don't know why, but it has.'

'Can't you just reboot it or something?' asked Molly.

'That's the thing. The door is airtight and sealed. Same for the elevator shaft. It's a safety measure against biological and chemical attacks.'

'Did you do this?' suggested Trey.

'No. I promise we didn't. The door has anti-hack protection so once it's gone into lock-down no-one's getting through. We've called the emergency services but they may need to get some heavy duty equipment to break you out. That could take up to six days though.'

'You've got to be fucking kidding!' said Trey.

'But you only have about forty minutes of air left. Before C02 build-up kills you.'

Seth was now conducting at multiple desktops. He'd pulled out the door's source code and busied himself dissecting it, running debugs, chipping away at the cause of the problem.

'But don't worry. We've got the world's greatest ever programmer looking into the issue,' Ella told the holographic representation of Molly and Trey. 'We're doing everything we can.'

'Found it,' Seth said, highlighting a block of code hovering above his desktop. 'I expected that to take considerably longer.'

Ella turned to the image of Molly and Trey. 'What did I tell you?' She smiled.

'Do I employ morons?' Seth said. Ella immediately cut the feed to the antechamber. He showed the block to Cyrus. It meant nothing to him. 'An invalid conditional "If, Then" loop. Human coding error as usual.'

'But you can fix it?'

'I've been working on something that will eliminate bugs such as this permanently,' Seth said proudly.

***

Trey and Molly sat on the floor of the antechamber trying to conserve air. The icy fingers of sleep slowly drawing a veil over their minds. Molly flicked at her off-line wrist-tab. The walls of the antechamber blocked all external electrical transmissions and without a signal she had no idea how long they had been trapped. The piece of dead plastic strapped to her arm exactly that. Trey, as expected from someone who campaigned for legislative human control of technology wore no tech.

Molly thought back to the months prior to this, when the ten million hit her account. The money could never ever replace her daughter. When Trey had suggested she use her high profile to increase awareness in his campaign it felt as if she may have a purpose again, although, right now, she regretted that decision.

***

Seth slapped his desktop, the holographic charms bobbing like boats in water across the workspace in response before settling.

'Yes! Done it.'

Ella approached him. 'You can get the door open?'

Seth looked at her, puzzled. He pulled a couple of charms closer, flicked them open and ran the program he'd written.

'Look at this,' Seth said as he stabbed at a number of input parameters with his finger.

'Seth, you're going to get the door open aren't you?'

'As technology gets more and more complex the capacity for logic errors increases. Beta testing just isn't rigorous enough to pick up every fault and there are too many time constraints to fully test every single scenario.'

'Seth…?'

'I've been working on this for some time but now I've finally cracked it.'

The holographic display rotated and turned. The words 'Hello World!' formed floating above his desktop. He beamed.

'The majority of programming bugs are due to simple human error. I've eliminated people from the coding process. This display is the output generated by a program coded by a program. Give it the conditions, functions and expected output and this app will write the code for you. Faster, and much more efficiently than any person could.'

'That will seriously reduce overheads, Seth. Fantastic! I'll begin a review of our development headcount,' said Cyrus.

'Seth,' Ella started. 'This will get the door open won't it? You said you would fix the problem.'

Seth turned to Ella, still not quite understanding.

'The problem with the door was the result of human error. This program will fix that. There'll never be any human coding bugs again. We can't get the door open, not once it's in lockdown but this,' he indicated the spinning words, 'will revolutionise the world.'

Ella turned to the gun-metal smart-door, aware of the two living souls behind it.

***

For Molly, every breath felt as if cotton wool was filling her lungs. She couldn't even contemplate speaking. Trey dozed peacefully in a corner of the antechamber and she envied him.

Ella's holographic image formed at the door, her eyes liquid. In the fuzziness of her thoughts Molly couldn't recall what it meant.

'I'm so sorry...' Ella began.

Vassalage

Denise Dyer

I roam the tired streets of Cardiff, they protect and hide me.

Once the city was colourful and exciting, it drew me in like a moth to a flame with so many veiled promises. Then I was an innocent country boy from a place where everyone knew my name.

Now it is my protector, I would never have believed I could vanish from view so easily. At a whim I can be seen or unseen, both angel and daemon, concealed by a city where nobody knows my name.

Decades ago I had a full head of hair and was considered handsome. Now my once golden sun-kissed skin shimmers from white to grey, and my blue eyes are dark and sunken in their sockets. My thin pale lips hide my broken uneven teeth. Teeth that make me grimace on the rare occasion that I smile. I have a taste for expensive well-tailored suits, they are my protector, hiding my empty shell of a body. To those of gothic persuasion I am heralded and held in awe, to others I am a freak.

My guilt eats away at me. I am glad that I have no need for sleep, as that is when I am faced with the reality of how I moved from one unholy war to another. Reliving every moment of my pitiful existence on the battlefields; the stench of death, the sight and smell of the trenches, and the unforgettable sounds of war.

Returning from war led to a downward spiral where I used

any means of sedation to try to give me release from the memories of what happened, begging anyone who would listen to release me and let me join my comrades, those I should have died with. I long to quieten those memories but an unforgiving voice in my head screams, 'Why did I survive?'

Now I watch the iniquitous as they realise that they must atone in death for what they did in life. Day after day, I try to convince myself that I am punishing those whose moral compass has gone awry, those who sate their dark hungers with unspeakable acts. When humanity has fled and left them soul-less without remorse, empty vessels heralding their own damnation, I see myself reflected in their eyes and know what fear is, yet I can no longer feel it.

Too late I realised the gilded cage I put myself into when I opened the box, the box that promised release and made me what I am, the Prince of Hell.

How I welcome my destruction, the void of emptiness must surely be better than this existence, yet for now in death as in life I am too much of a coward to face my own demise.

I take solace in my continual torture. The torment is a shroud enfolding me in its drapes.

I deserve this and must endure my hell-bound Heart.

HAIKU
Spring to Summer

Angela Edwards

Cherry tree blossoms
at the pavement by my door
winter finishing

Gorse in the car park
golden as buttercups
bunting of spring

Cherry petals fall
having waited through winter
for one flower burst

White petals
falling like snow
summer next

The horse chestnut tree
on the corner of the street
Lights its candles

Lace of wild chervil
decorates the park
With embroidery

A Moonlit Letter

Pip Pryor

Every night I see you, my Moon, up there in the void sky with your infinite sisters. All identical, but I know you are mine. Nobody could mistake your radiance; a candle flame guiding me to my true purpose.

You make it hard to reach you – I know this, my Moon. This desolate expanse that divides us, air too thin and winds too mighty for me to fly through. But this distance is what makes my craving grow. Perhaps you think me a fool, but I know these games you play. You are testing me! See if I will give up and fly on. You send me false prophets – dazzling, flickering idols – that singe my antennae and burn my wings. In that moment, how real they seem, capturing a glimmer of your sweet, honeyed radiance. I will admit, I have been fooled once or twice – keeping secrets from you benefits no-one under your brilliant gaze – but those times I have been burned, I know you have designed it so, my Moon, to punish me for my infidelity. Who am I to share that sacred dance; the secrets of proximity with another – the one we have reserved for each other when you finally grant me our fated meeting? An utter fool, that is what I am, and each new burn that scorns my scales I know is rightfully deserved for my insolence.

And that is to speak nothing of the goliaths you send, my Moon! They chase me down with hammers of plastic, trying to crush me against the walls, hellbent on my early destruction. I have seen the shadows of my brethren: mangled, dust-coloured halos, and once even saw the act in action. Such a narrow escape I made! As tragic as it is, they are the failures – a grim reminder of what will await me if my devotion ever wavers. But I am different. I am strong! You send these goliaths to train me, push me to my physical pinnacle – and I have been pushed! It would not suit you to allow someone so weak and pitiful to join your side.

So, I pray you hear my cries, my Moon! For despite how beautiful you are in all your morning dew glory, I can only bear to admire you from such a distance for so long until my heart aches. But I cannot be so greedy, my Moon, for you always preferred the humble.

Forever awaiting,

Your Moth.

Galaxy Lamp

Nejra Ćehić

I buy an exquisite lamp at the flea market. A spherical lamp made of multi-coloured glass. Most of my belongings are functional; this lamp is purely decorative. It has a working bulb, in that it produces light, but the light would be too weak to write or read by. Nor do I have space for the lamp in my flat. Everything has its place. This lamp will have a place in my future home – a home with a room dedicated to nothing but sitting in the soft light and dreaming. I will stare at the colours and savour the silence like a sweetness on my tongue, teasing time between my fingertips.

'What time is it?'

I turn to see a young man next to me on the train platform, looking at his phone. Before I can respond, he puts it back to his ear.

'It's OK, I'm early. The train's coming in… six minutes.'

I look across at the opposite platform and count eight people. We are the only two on ours. More people heading into the city than out.

'I'm tired, yeah. But good. You OK, babes?'

He's got nothing on him but his phone. Men always move through life so unencumbered.

I'm rarely without a bag on my shoulder and a bag in hand. Two bags in hand today.

'Nah, don't worry about them. Why, what did she say?'

He has a nice voice. Gentle but resonant.

'Listen, I can't have problems. I've changed, babes. I'm gonna be there for Tyler.'

His son? Daughter? Another family member? Friend?

'I'm with you. I wanna get away from here, there's too many negative people. Me and you, we're going places. America. Spain. Australia. South Africa!'

Pretty unimaginative destinations, I think, even as I find myself wishing he would take me with him. I'm staring at him, but he's absorbed in his conversation and staring at the train tracks. I look away, embarrassed that one of the eight people on the platform opposite might have noticed my interest in this stranger.

'You've always been there for me, babes. You know when you was little, and you'd be in your room scared of the dark, and then your mum would come in and put on the galaxy lamp? And you'd just be there looking at the cool lights and feeling like someone loved you? That's like what happened in my life when we met.

'Babes, don't cry. I'll see you later, yeah? We're gonna be cool. I love you. I love you.'

He puts the phone in his pocket. Then he gets it out and looks at it again. Looks up at the sky. A sky without a single cloud, bird, plane trail; nothing for the eyes to encounter, for the mind to meditate on. He turns his face towards me. A face with everything for the eyes and the mind.

'Sorry if I was talking too loud.'

I want to reply but I can only manage a shrug of the shoulders and a smile with which I intend to communicate 'no problem at all'. I can't find words because I'm too busy taking in his teeth, his skin, his eyes. Especially his eyes, their light flashing and fading against deep and infinite obscurity.

I sense movement in my periphery and see the train

approaching in the distance. He turns and starts walking towards it, slowly at first, then faster. Stops. Then starts walking again. I was hoping we'd be in the same carriage. I want to see his face again. Maybe we'll get off at the same station, start chatting, become friends, more than friends… even though he's in love with someone else.

He's almost at the end of the platform. I'll probably never see him again, I think with regret. The image of him in my mind is already less clear. I'm looking down at a pool, his face is looking up at me from beneath the surface of the water.

He jumps in front of the train.

My bags hit the platform.

I hear my lamp shatter.

Stitched up

*Winner of the Cardiff Writers' Circle 75
word flash fiction competition 2022*

Peter Gaskell

Yara learned embroidery at the refugee camp because creating something beautiful stopped her from thinking too much and calmed her.

Selling her skilful work, the charity gave her money to support her sisters still in Syria.

Her most beautiful dress yet, this one Yara imagined wearing after she reached Europe.

"You said I could sail tomorrow?"

The man promising her safe sea passage smiled as he folded another of her battered banknotes into his pocket.

Dates

Sara Hayes

He turned his back
on kind and comfortable
chose the unsettling
unpredictable one
hoping she would
rewild him
but years on
they have three meals a day
and a diary
open
on the kitchen table
to help them
remember
their places

The Man, The Girl, and The Goblin

Leusa Lloyd

A rustle outside woke her suddenly. The snap of a branch and the sound of heavy footsteps approaching. She pressed herself against the wall of the cave, arms hugging her knees to her chest, her eyes watching the cave entrance in fear. All the animals that it could be flashed across her mind's eye: wolves, lions, cackling hyenas. But when the creature strode into the fire-lit cavern, she was surprised to find no wings, fur, or fangs. He looked just like her, but different. He was taller, with smooth, rosy flesh. His shoulders were broad, and his arms and legs were thick with muscles. His breasts were much flatter than hers, but shapely. His hair was long and inky, and progressed down to his chin and upper lip. But his eyes – they glowed like a scarlet flame.

She was overcome by his beauty and gazed at him in awe. The Man's red eyes met hers, and she felt suspended in his gaze. Without a flicker of acknowledgement crossing his face, he turned to leave.

'No,' she said, and made to follow him. With one swift movement the Man turned and struck her across the face with the back of his hand. It was so forceful that she fell to the floor, clutching her cheek. She quickly got up and ran out of the cave after him, but he'd already disappeared into the night air. She returned to the cave and sobbed all night in despair.

A few moons passed until the crocus peaked through the muddy Earth, and the forest creatures had awoken from their slumber. The Girl travelled from the forest to brooks and hills. In the day, she continued to hunt, bathe and collect firewood, but with the soft fall of darkness the same familiar sadness crept in. One Spring morning, she came across a clearing in the trees, where there was a large lake, filled with silvery water. As she got closer, her eyes grew wide with astonishment, because there he was: the creature from the cave. He was standing in the lake up to his waist, rubbing water over his shimmering skin to wash away the dirt. Slowly, she walked towards him. After a few steps he turned to look at her, his scarlet eyes transfixed on her in a piercing gaze. She saw some of his furs and possessions at the edge of the lake, and with them an ivory comb. She picked it up from the ground, and then carefully climbed into the water, wading towards him until she stood within touching distance. Then, she shakily raised the comb to his beard. He made no sound or movement, but his eyes did not leave hers. Once she had combed his beard, she moved around him to his long, wet hair, carefully brushing out all the knots. Then she braided it into one long plait, tying the bottom with string she fashioned from a nearby reed.

When she had finished, he silently made his way to the shore, and put on his furs. He gathered up his belongings and turned to leave. She splashed out of the water, running after him. Just as she was about to reach him, he swiftly turned and struck her across the face. She felt her cheek smack into the cold ground, tasted metallic blood on her lips. She lifted her head just in time to see him stride away, back turned.

As the days passed the leaves withered and dropped. Before long, a blanket of thick white snow covered the ground again, and a fierce blizzard raged. The Girl hauled herself up in her furs inside the cave and stayed close to the fire. She only left it in search of food or wood. One day, once the snowstorm had subsided slightly, she ventured out hunting. She was crouched down behind the bare trees skinning a rabbit when she heard it: a whimper of pain. The Girl whipped round, and gasped. Slumped against a fallen tree, shivering fiercely, was the Man. He had a deep gash across his torso, blood spilling onto the ground, luminescent against the clean ivory of the snow. As she approached, he raised his bowed head slightly and she felt his watchful scarlet eyes upon her once more.

She bent down to look at his wound, but then suddenly in the distance she heard a wolf howl. Snowflakes begin to fall, thick and fast, and she could feel in the air that there would be another storm.

'Quickly,' she hissed, and manoeuvred her body under his right shoulder, pushing up as he rose to his feet. They staggered through the trees, moving as fast as they could. Sometimes she slipped, but she quickly recomposed herself, ushering him forward. When they reached the cave, she breathed a sigh of relief, and put wood on the fire, the flames bursting into a roar. The Man lay next to them, violently shaking as his body responded to the heat. She cleaned his wound and rubbed a green paste made of plants onto it and covered him with furs. Hours later, when he had awoken from a deep sleep, she patiently fed him lumps of cooked rabbit meat, held a cup of water to his lips. He fell asleep again, but now hot, sweaty, clammy. He wouldn't wake and his breaths were shallow.

He stayed like this for many days. She tended to him, cleaning his wound, and feeding him in his brief flashes of consciousness. She didn't leave his side, and eventually ran so low on food she barely ate.

By the time the ice thawed, the Man began to wake more

frequently. His temperature had returned to normal. But he was still very weak. She began leaving him to go hunting, bringing back squirrels, rabbits, and deer, sometimes carrots and potatoes if she found them. Soon, he could sit upright, then he could stand and walk short distances. By the time the days had stretched out to be long and scorching, he had been restored to full health.

One morning he awoke, felt a small sunbeam streaming through the entrance of the cave warm his cheek. He was strong: his wound had healed to a salmon-coloured scar. He got up and walked towards the entrance. He crossed the threshold of the cave and paused, placing his feet firmly into the ground – these were the first steps outside he'd taken outside since the harsh Winter. He took a breath, drawing the air deep into his lungs. He smelt the moss and the pines, tasted the saltwater of the distant sea on his tongue, heard the clamouring of the birds. He took another step forward, and another, and began to walk away.

The Girl saw this from where she was sitting inside the cave, she got up and ran after him in a panic. When she was close enough, she reached out to him, brushing her fingertips against his back. As swift as a swallow he turned and struck her to the ground. Without hesitation he carried on walking.

She scrambled back to her feet. 'Wait,' she cried, clutching her purple cheek as hot tears stung her eyes. She ran in front of him and stood there, staring him in the face. His ruby eyes flashed at her, as he stopped.

'What will it take, to make you want me?'

'Give me something,' he spat at her, 'something no man could ever give me, that I could never take for myself.'

'But you are strong,' she spluttered, 'you are clever. You can swim, you can climb, you can run. There is nothing on this Earth I can give you that you cannot take for yourself.'

He looked at her, then pushed past her and walked away. She watched his figure fade into the darkness of the forest. The Girl fell to the floor, wailing, her body spasming and convulsing with the force of her cries, her hands clawing at the dirt beneath her. Her golden hair fell about her in a wild mess, covering her face.

'I can help you,' she heard a soft voice chime. Her head snapped up and she looked around, but she couldn't see where the voice had come from.

'Who... who's there?' Her voice shook.

A small figure emerged from behind a nearby oak tree. A knee-height man, his skin was green and slimy, like a toad. Boils covered his small face, and two beady black eyes were set deep into it. His fingers were long and slender, the nails yellow and hooked. He wore a little woollen shirt, and on his feet, red shoes with tips that turn upwards.

The Girl gawked at him in amazement.

'What... what are you?' she gasped. She'd never seen a creature like him before.

'I'm a Goblin,' he replied in a scratchy voice, 'and I can help you give the Man what he wants. But... there will be a price.'

'Yes!' the Girl replied through sobs, her breath ragged. 'I'll give you anything. Name your price, and it is yours.'

'I want your blood.' The Goblin stared at her with his onyx eyes. 'Every full moon, your breasts will swell, your back will ache, your hair will become tangled and your skin will break out in boils, and you will scream with pain for seven whole nights as you bleed. Then you will return to how you are now, until the next full moon. This will happen for forty Summers. It is a small price, lady,' the Goblin smiled menacingly.

'Yes,' said the Girl, wiping her eyes, 'I'll do it.'

With this the Goblin began an incantation in a low voice, in a language she didn't understand. Dark clouds gathered above them, and the trees trembled as thunder rumbled in the distance. The Goblin danced around her in a circle, his chants getting louder and louder. Suddenly, the girl was struck by a great flash of light from the sky. The Girl screamed and writhed in pain. Her stomach swelled to triple its size, as the muscles in her pelvis ripped apart, one tendon at a time. As she howled, rain fell from the black clouds, and the Goblin began to laugh, a sickening hyena cackle. The Girl felt her body begin to expand and contract as the pain intensified. She threw her head back and screeched an almighty scream, and, from deep within, heaved an almighty push. Then, everything went dark...

When she awoke, the clouds had cleared, and the Goblin had gone. At her feet, she saw a bundle of furs. She picked it up and within the bundle lay a tiny creature – it looked just like her, but smaller. The baby began to wail, and she instinctively picked it up, clutched it to her bosom. She then raced through the forest, looking for the Man. She found him in a small clearing, roasting a wild boar on a spit. She slowed to a walk, and he turned around to gaze upon her, with his red eyes. She laid the baby down at his feet.

'Your gift,' she said.

He paused, bent down, then scooped the baby up in his large arms. He stared down at it, its tiny arms and features. The baby opened his eyes, revealing two russet irises. But his hair was flaxen.

'It's a boy,' said the Man, surprised. 'You've given me another man.' His features softened.

From that day on, the Man and the Boy were inseparable. The Man hunted tigers and fashioned the Boy's clothes from their furs. The Man taught the Boy how to hunt, fish, swim and climb trees. Man took a willow and made him a bow and arrow. Man built his own cave out of stone and called it a 'house'. The Boy grew big and strong, and soon he was as tall as Man, and his muscles as thick. Boy's hair was long and blond, and shone like buttercups. His irises remained blood-red. Man and Boy roamed the forests and the hills and the sands, hunting and eating, laughing together, and watching the stars shine in the black sky.

When they roamed, The Girl trailed behind them, limply. Then, once their house was built, the Man chained her up inside. Nobody looked or spoke to her. The Man greeted her each morning with a strike across the face. She cooked their food and cleaned their furs while they were out. She cried silently to herself in the darkness, which became worse as the full moon approached, as she knew the agony it would bring for her. Not a soul heard her, apart from the Goblin, who came once a month to collect his payment.

Daffodils

Angela Edwards

Angled at the ceiling
trumpet mouths shout at me
of cold fields in rows,
the unravelling of bulbs
to green points
for a single purpose.

Cut to travel as buds
in elastic bands and priced
in the supermarket box.
we met for a pound.

Here they expand and burst
to a sun's corona
beyond the battering of bees
shouting at me with trumpet mouths
that they've made it!

A Village Legend

Sara Hayes

Barley harvested, Songlong declared to the other village leaders,
'We should celebrate! A festival! I'll supply the goat.'

Li hadn't lived here long. He hadn't grown up with these men and women, didn't know the community's funny stories and whispered tragedies. It made a difference, he thought, kept him apart. Tonight he would try to fit in.

In the lanterns' flaming light, acrobats tumbled, clowns skipped, laughing and teasing, his friends danced to the drum beat, clapped hands and sang. There were nuts, berries, fish, sweet dumplings and infusions of herbs. Smells of cooking filled the smoky air.

Li noticed a scuffle amongst the musicians. One of them, Chunlye, was holding the clay xun Li had made. It had been challenging making the flat-bottomed bottle with finger holes, tapered neck and lower lip rest.

'Li,' called Chunlye. 'The xun you made, it's broken!'

The music stopped. The players, moaning and grumpy, gathered around Li.

'What's wrong? Is it cracked?' asked Li.

'Don't know. Listen!'

Chunlye blew. The only sound was his rasping breath.

'See, it doesn't work!'

Li took the object gingerly. The light was too poor to check for hairline cracks. He tried blowing. He couldn't make it sing but he became aware of water dribbling through his fingers.

'Hey!' he exclaimed.

Chunlye seized the xun and poured the remaining water over Li's head, laughing hysterically.

Li shrieked at the sting of cold water and then grinned. He was contributing to the village legends. He really did belong now.

My Heroine

Eliane Huss

So many great names to choose from
The Marys, the Beths and the Annes
But what about you?
Yes you,
Who didn't make it into the public eye,
Forgotten in history,
No monument
And often no name on a grave.
Yes you
Woman, Mother, Grandmother
Keeping the fire going
Cooking and cleaning
Minding the children, men and parents
Toiling the fields, farms and factories
While men play war.
Tending to the sick, wounded and dead.
Often disregarded and oppressed
Yet always protecting the next generation
From stones, spears and bullets.
You are my real heroine.
Thanks to you
I am.

Ithaca

Stephen Pritchard

Lunchtime, and the restaurant was crowded, the waiter apologetic: 'Sorry, m'sieur, there is only this table.'

Just my luck. I'd be a finger-smear away from four kids, the nearest, with mayo-daubed chin, tearing apart a langoustine. And I was wearing freshly laundered cream chinos.

The father, built like a rugby forward, spread his hands apologetically, huge hands with broken nails. 'Sorry, we must be your worst nightmare.'

'No problem,' I lied, and smiled as I lied.

I ordered the dorade and a vin blanc and opened my book. But Homer and Odysseus proved, for the moment, less interesting than my neighbours. 'Mayo-chops' had inherited the father's curly black hair. The elder girl the deep corn-coloured locks of the mother. The youngest were also a boy/girl black/blonde combo. All were sucking and slurping from the two-tiered plateau des fruits de mer. I watched the mother slide an oyster into her raised mouth and, eyes half-closed, swallow, slowly, luxuriously. A bright, direct voice broke my reverie.

'Do you think my mummy is pretty?'

The elder girl regarded me expectantly. Her mother intervened. 'Zoe, that's rude. Apologise to the gentleman.'

Zoe was not to be quelled. 'Alright, I'm sorry. But I asked nicely. And he was looking at you.'

The waiter served my fish and wine. Before filleting the

dorade I admitted, 'Your daughter was quite right. I was admiring you, enjoying your fruits de mer, all of you.'

I might have added that I didn't think the mother was pretty. She undoubtedly had been pretty. How could she not have been, with that heart-shaped face, riot of blonde hair, and those bluer than blue eyes? But a trace of something, gravitas, experience, in the set of her lips, the line of her jaw, had taken her beyond pretty. She was handsome. Perhaps beautiful.

Now she asked, 'Are you on holiday?'

I temporised. 'Just a few days. I don't like being away too long.'

The father, expertly extracting the claw meat from a lobster, asked, 'Away from what? Or who?'

'Whom' I corrected him silently before replying, 'Oh, normal stuff. Home. Work. Nothing complicated.'

They weren't entitled to know that I was here, in the south of France, only because my mother had died recently.

The woman had the pretty laugh of a teenager. 'We've usually found "complicated" is good.'

'Mayo-chops' jerked a bulot from its shell and liquid speckled the cover of my book. I fiddled defensively with a napkin and returned the mother's question. 'Are you on holiday?'

'God no. We've nowhere to be on holiday from.'

I shook my head. 'Is that what you mean by complicated?'

The husband shrugged. 'It's pretty simple. We're rootless. Wanderers on the face of the earth.'

'You mean, like, hippies?'

The mother wagged her blonde head. 'Not at all like hippies. Like nomads. Lewis builds dry-stone walls. We go wherever the work is. He's been renewing the terraces in some local vineyards.'

'Really? I didn't know they taught that in college.'

Lewis raised an eyebrow and laughed. 'College? No chance. Didn't even make it as far as GCSEs.'

A glance arced between the couple. I felt the force-field surrounding them, like electricity, or pins and needles. Those blue, blue eyes turned towards me.

'Lewis was taught by Luca, a wonderful old guy we met in Croatia. He was over eighty and still dry-stone walling. He wanted someone he could train up so the craft wouldn't die out. There was nowhere else we needed to be so Lewis became Luca's pupil. We named our first-born,' indicating 'Mayo-chops', 'Luca, in honour of Old Luca.'

Lewis nodded. 'It was the least we could do. Besides, Luca means "he who gives his light to others".'

'And you make a living at it?'

'You'd be surprised. I get commissions from all over. There're so few of us around.'

'And, darling, because, like Old Luca said, you're a natural.'

'Aye, Annabel, lass, Yorkshire born and bred,' exaggerating his slight Northern accent, 'like as not dry-stone walls are in my DNA.' Reverting to his usual voice he said reverently, 'Luca was a great teacher. The best.'

Putting down her wine glass the mother, Annabel, added, 'If it wasn't for Old Luca we wouldn't be here now. Or heading to Greece next.'

'Greece?' I asked.

Lewis was matter of fact. 'A heritage fund is commissioning me to renew a dry-stone revetment that's threatening to collapse and tumble an ancient Byzantine church into the valley below.'

Annabel came in again. 'We're especially excited because the church is on,' she pointed at the cover of my book, 'Ithaca.'

'Ithaca? Really? Perhaps you'll stop your wanderings and stay there, like Odysseus.'

Luca, wiping mayo from his chin with the back of his hand, shook his head vigorously.

'That's not right. Odysseus leaves his island, Ithaca, and spends ten years fighting the Trojan War, then another ten years voyaging and having adventures before he gets home again, but he can't stay there, he has to take his oar and go on travelling until he finds a land where the people don't use salt and don't know what his oar is.' Pausing for breath, and to suck a mussel from its shell, Luca looked across at me. 'How weird is that? It must mean…'

His mother laid a hand on his arm. 'Let's leave the rest of the story for another time, darling. And what do we know about talking with our mouth full?'

Luca muttered, 'Sorry; but I thought he would be interested.'

'Oh, I am,' I cut in, 'I've always thought the whole point of the story was Odysseus's homecoming.'

Luca's eyes were nut brown, like his father's. 'The best stories always end in a sort of mystery.'

'Do they? I prefer things precise, exact.'

Lewis' judicious, 'It takes all sorts,' prompted my cautious, 'But maybe Luca's right, perhaps I could do with a bit of mystery in my life. I'll have to think about it.'

'It's not about thinking,' Annabel's voice, soft with encouragement, 'it's about feeling.'

I ate the last of my frites, centred my knife and fork on the plate and, making conversation, remarked, 'I see what you mean about complicated. Chasing the work. Croatia, France, Greece. Here, there, everywhere. And four young kids in tow. Must be tough.'

'That's not at all how we look at it. But I understand it wouldn't suit everyone.'

Her reproof was gentle, but a reproof nonetheless. She was probably a few years older than Lewis. And, attractive, even beautiful, as she was, I felt you wouldn't want to cross her.

Lewis looked at her fondly. 'Annabel is a painter. A good one. She sells mostly through a couple of galleries in Oslo and Helsinki.'

'I'm just lucky the cold North seems to like my reminders of the warm South.'

'Where did you go to art school?' I asked.

She shook her head, blonde locks shimmering. 'Formal education's not the only way of becoming what you want to be. Let alone discovering what you need to be.'

It was another reproof. And there was more.

'I started off as a good girl. Compliant. Did as I was told. School. University. Then teaching. But I knew I was on a dead-end street. Until,' her voice warmed, 'Lewis and I fell in love. And nothing could ever be the same again. An over-used expression. But it happens to be true in our case. We had nothing and everything. Somewhere along the way I discovered how to paint.'

I waited, but she had said as much as she was going to. Lewis elaborated. 'Until Old Luca sorted me out it was Alice's painting that put food on our table.' Leaning across she placed a hand on his. 'But before that, at the beginning, you did all sorts. Labouring. Cleaning. Caretaking. It worked out because we stayed true to each other.'

Zoe piped up, 'Lunch is taking an awfully long time. And we've finished our ice-creams. Can we go to the beach now?'

The two youngest, they'd been so quiet I'd forgotten their existence, bellowed,

'Beeeachhh.'

'You've been very patient,' said Lewis, 'off you go. We'll be a few more minutes. Stay out of the sea until we get there.'

Annabel cleaned the kids' faces with napkins, then they slipped off their chairs and each shook hands with me, Luka even saying, 'Nice to have met you, sir.' Astonished, I managed to respond in kind. Racing to the edge of the café terrace they leapt, arms and legs extended like four skinny starfish, onto the beach.

Annabel tucked a wad of euros into an empty wine glass and the couple stood up to leave. I stood too.

She slid out from her side of the table. Her dark-blue linen dress, scoop-necked and sleeveless, the long skirt slit to mid-thigh, displayed her golden-gleaming arms, shoulders and leg. In a few years she might be considered too mature for such a revealing dress. For now though, she was magnificent.

'I hope Ithaca works out for you.'

'It already has,' she replied. 'Make sure your Ithaca works for you.'

'You're getting complicated again,' I said.

'It's simple. It's what Luca told you.'

'About Ithaca not being the end of Odysseus's wanderings?'

'Exactly. Ithaca is where you start from. Ithaca's gift is the journey. You just need the courage, or desperation, to accept the gift.'

'And that's what you did?'

Lewis slid an arm round her waist. 'We had no choice. We were in love; that upset other people so we weighed anchor and set sail on our own.'

'I don't understand.'

Annabel's lips brushed my cheek and she confided, 'We've told you all we're going to, and all you need to know.'

Hand in hand they set out to reclaim their children.

Putting on my sunglasses I sat down, mind whirling.

Are they really fugitives? A teacher and her pupil? But they'd have to have been ten years on the run. At least. Yet he's an internationally-known builder of dry-stone walls. She's a successful, self-taught artist. And, between them, making a more than reasonable living.

That plateau de fruits de mer is the most expensive item on the menu. And four kids. So how does that work? And the kids so formal, so polite, so, old-fashioned. You said it, Luca, a mystery, a total, bloody mystery.

'Dessert, m'sieur?' The waiter hovered. I shook my head but ordered a digestif. I was about to need it even more than I realised.

***

'Time somebody got you off your arse.'

The chair opposite me was occupied. I removed my sunglasses. To make sure.

'Mother?'

'Close your mouth. You look idiotic.'

'It can't be you.'

'That's for you to decide.'

'You died, six months ago.'

'And left you with everything; except an excuse.'

'An excuse? For what?'

'For not getting off your arse and making something of your life.'

'I had to take care of you.'

'And now I'm gone. And you're free.'

'There's still my career.'

'Career? Don't make me laugh. A job is what you've got. One you've been stuck in for twenty years. And will be for another twenty, 'less you do something about it.'

'It's not that simple.'

'It is if you decide it is.'

'You sound like that Annabel and Lewis couple.'

'Maybe you should listen to us then. But don't take too bloody long about it.'

'It's not really you, is it?'

This time there was no answer. And nobody sitting across the table from me. I looked around. I was the only customer left in the restaurant. The waiter brought my bill.

'Is it too late to order a carafe of white wine?' I asked.

'Un carafe, m'sieur? Bien sur. I will bring it to you on the terrasse.'

An afternoon of wine and Homer was the best idea I'd had for ages. And I wouldn't think; about anything. I'd surrender to feelings, to complications. Discover whether I had the courage, or the desperation, to accept the gift of Ithaca.

Two Floors Below

David Thomas

Two floors below, a wake for a war hero.

I'm under the roof beams, springing the catch on his forbidden war chest. Inside, a soldier's simple effects and the medals of a family icon. But what's this, an envelope, postmarked Rio, 1946. My German is poor, but 'nützlich information', 'heimlich', 'danke' and the bundle of Reichmarks tell their own story. I'm stunned beyond belief. Forbidden indeed!

But I miss the envelope from the British government.

My Red Lines

Sara Hayes

My red lines are not immovable boundaries.

They are pencils in a jar and
baby pictures on my fridge,
plastic bricks under a kitchen chair
coming out the other side
ending abruptly at the wall.

They are bands around the fold-over tops
of my brother's grey school socks and
the knotted stuff of his red jumper.

They stay under the words my computer doesn't like
or I don't know how to spell,
making me think again.

They guide me when I am not sure of the way,
trunk roads, footpaths, contours on a map,
Central Line on the Underground,
Hanover's Red Thread, three miles long.

I've seen them on earthworms, cinnabar moths,
choughs' legs and red panda tails,
rust tears falling from railings,

the operation scar on my daughter's chest.

They are what my cat did to me when I came too close.

These are my history's relish.
I have other flavours too.

Kitchen Drinks – Slinger

Lesley James

He knows the etymology of Grenadine

The Japanese Jack Rose
unfolds like Guerlain perfume
or a Transformer

Others, brown, thuggish, thump
the tongue in absinthe whiskiness
You need two hands for the glass

Spreadsheets map the stocks of
tinctures in the Linenfold oak
cupboard that once held a television

He knows the etymology of Falernum
He is the Real Maraschino

Martinis

dry martinis are not a vice they're essential
like MERRING, one of those conditions
we consider biologically necessary
for life: a whiff of extra-dry
(Martini never Dolin)
four parts gin
a deftly
cut
s
l
i
v
e
r
of
lemon zest, its oil spritzed
like petrol floating on puddles

A Crisis of Singularity

Peter Gaskell

All-inclusive, his guest status clearly identifiable by the plastic bracelet they strapped round his wrist at Reception; blue, the coolest of colours, it reinforced the calm he felt now his holiday was circumscribed by predictability. All-inclusive meant everything he might need would be available within the confines of this hotel. OK, the food choice might get boring but the important thing was Stephen felt safe.

Arlene though would have preferences of her own and he should have reckoned for these. But it had all been a last-minute rush to book. Getting the Thomson deal meant sharing and Stephen had been hard-pressed to find a companion for the holiday. Freshly arrived from Australia, he knew Arlene only as the latest reader to join his international book club. That they preferred different fiction genres should have indicated their differences but as the price was irresistible, they agreed to share the twin room holiday package. On a platonic basis, naturally.

All went to plan till the fourth day, although their compatibility was first challenged when their rep presented the company's coach tour options. A girl from the outback, Arlene was attracted by a trip to the sand dunes, an unusual feature for a tropical island. She had paid for the excursion before Stephen had digested its unsettling implications for their all-inclusive deal. Arlene was sure there would be a decent bar at the beach on the far side of the dunes.

After a three-hour drive, they were dropped in a village square across the island where the coach would collect them at 7pm, just after sunset which they could watch over the sea from a high point in the dunes.

Only a few square miles in area, bounded by the sea and a road, for agoraphobic Stephen this might as well be the Sahara. In a group though, Stephen felt safe enough. A breeze blowing off the sea cooled their faces as they marched up and down the shifting dunes into the midday sun, the sand surprisingly firm, its warmth inviting the walkers to go barefoot. Stephen reluctantly followed the others in removing his shoes but declined Arlene's invitation to roll down the side of a dune with her.

Reaching the beach, they found Paddy's Bar where several of the group sat down at tables outside and ordered lunch. Washing their enchilada down with Guinness, they watched the windsurfers and, at Arlene's suggestion again, traded rounds of drinks on bets as to which surfer would stay upright longest. Last to leave the bar to head back toward the dunes, Stephen and Arlene became further distracted as they passed through an area reserved for nude bathers.

Or rather Arlene did. She removed her top and invited Stephen to strip if only to blend with their surroundings. He declined. As they lay on the sand, he dozed while his companion relayed her giggling commentary on the men self-consciously strutting their prowess around them.

Stephen opened his eyes. The sun had now dipped behind a cloud low on the horizon. Arlene was no longer lying next to him. Spotting her by the water's edge chatting to a naked bather, he padded over.

'Arlene, we'll miss the coach unless we go now.'

'OK, just give us a minute, would you, Stevie?'

111

Sat on the sand a few feet from Arlene, he waited and watched as her companion pointed her toward a garish advert nearby for tonight's big party at Club el Gogo. Arlene caught Stephen's eye but gave no signal that she intended to extricate herself.

Stephen got up and headed inland. Climbing a dune he watched the sun set, fat and orange across the sparkling sea before he trudged down the other side. He was unsure he was holding a straight line as he ascended the next, disappointed he couldn't see the rendezvous point, just more featureless dunes under the pinkening sky.

Uncertainty began conspiring with fear of the boundless space around him to arouse the panic he often felt when out of his comfort zone. Palpitating, sweating and nauseous now, he cursed Arlene as he descended into a deep hollow where he tried to recover his composure. He would carry on through the gathering darkness, though whether in the right direction he could only hope and guess.

Hearing just the wind and seeing nothing but endless sand as he scaled another dune, he sensed the space around and above converge to form a weight that seemed bent on crushing his spirit and his will to continue. Dizzy and trembling he retched, sinking to his knees to stain the golden sand brown with his vomit.

'Well, you didn't get very far, did you?' came a voice out of the wind. It was Arlene. 'I figured you'd have been able to ask the coach driver to wait. Too late now I guess.'

After the exertion of vomiting, Stephen paused before responding.

'Not on your way to the nightclub then?'

'Well, I would've but...'

'I hope you asked him why he chose pink to dye his pubes.'

Arlene laughed. 'You didn't realise he was gay? Anyway, seeing all bared on a beach isn't what turns me on.'

She paused for a reaction but none came.

'You're shaking. You OK?'

Still Stephen could say nothing. Arlene held out her hand to help him up but he refused it.

'Did you hear about the guy who got lost in the Aussie desert? His jeep broke down and he had to walk the rest of the way. They found his body a few metres from his jeep. He'd been walking for hours in circles.'

'With no landmarks to orient me, what did you expect?'

Arlene pointed to Venus, bright above the horizon. 'The evening star's in the west so you could've oriented and found the village by now.'

'I don't know the heavens, Arlene. It's all so scarily empty up there I don't look.'

By the time they reached the village, the sky was ablaze with stars. As they'd feared, the coach had gone. Arlene watched Stephen slump onto the churchyard wall and drop his head into his hands.

'Right, Stephen, we're not going to let this get us down. The first thing to do is raise our heads and look up. It's like we've got millions of friends out there. Just get connected, will you?'

Stephen paused. Before he could discover whether panic or wonder at the starry firmament would prevail, he noticed a light was on in the church.

'Let's go in,' he said.

Inside they found it empty but for an elderly woman praying in the corner. They waited. At last she stood up and turned to face them, with a question in Spanish. They didn't understand so Arlene gesticulated their intention to get to their resort. Come, she gesticulated back, follow me. She led them down the road to a house where she knocked. A burly islander came to the door and stared at them expressionlessly.

'Taxi,' said the woman.

'Dondé?' asked the man.

'Varapalomas,' she replied.

The taxi driver avoided any eye contact as he gestured to his car, a 1950s Cadillac, before rubbing his thumb and fingers.

'Fifty dollars – US.'

Stephen pulled all he had out of his wallet and handed forty dollars to him. The driver looked at Arlene who shook her head, suggesting she had no money. The man grunted before going back inside to get his keys. When he returned, he was accompanied by a wolfish-looking teenager who got into the front passenger seat. Arlene and Stephen were ushered into the back. The old Cadillac groaned into life and heaved off along the dark road. With no response to their attempts at conversation, Stephen began to sweat and palpitate again.

Arlene put her hand on his. 'Don't worry,' she said. 'You could see how devout the old lady was. She wouldn't have set us up just so these two would rob us.' Stephen extricated his hand and placed hers on her knee.

With no moon, outside the village all they could see was the broken road stretching away in the headlights. The car's suspension was a boon at least, alleviating their discomfort from the worst potholes. Then, without notice, the driver pulled to a stop in the middle of nowhere and indicated they should get out. Panic seized Stephen again. They already had all his cash, now it would be Arlene's turn to empty her purse. Then what – a knife in the dark? But the driver didn't follow them out of the car. Instead he waved some official document at them and promptly drove off, their isolation on the dark road witnessed only by the constellations overhead.

They walked on in silence, shivering in their beachwear, Stephen abject and still furious at his companion while Arlene nursed her guilt about her insensitivity toward Stephen's condition and her dalliance at the beach. It was half an hour before a vehicle came by. They stuck out their thumbs but it didn't stop.

Again Stephen felt the oppressiveness of the space around him, yet this time their abandonment made it worse. In the dunes, endless sand and sky had conspired to summon his agoraphobic demons but they had flown off on the wind when Arlene appeared. Now they were back, as if bolstered by confidence Arlene was in league with them. Stephen again wanted to cuss Arlene but couldn't.

Then something cracked. Becoming so insignificant in the landscape these past hours had shrunken Stephen's sense of self; condensing it to such a point the burden of it was intolerable. Looking heavenward at last, his fate seemed to mirror that of a failing star, spent of its fuel and collapsing, himself no longer a multi-dimensional human being but a singularity, at the centre of some black hole with monumental mass. First though, and now he almost felt the urge to laugh, shouldn't there have been a supernova, a blast of the star's outer layers at colossal speed into space?

And so he couldn't help himself. 'This is your fucking fault, Arlene,' he yelled. 'Posing around the beach for hours when we should have been heading back to the village with the others.'

Arlene was stunned by his uncharacteristic outburst.

'Christ, Stevie, keep your hair on. I'm here to have fun too you know.'

The sound of a car coming round the bend in their direction gagged his reply. As it approached, Stephen darted across the road, forcing it to a screeching halt. The driver jumped out and swore at Stephen in Spanish.

'It's no use cussing me, hombre. I don't sodding speak the lingo.'

'Then how the hell did you beach-bums get to be on this road after dark? Where's your permit?'

The man's colloquial English took him aback.

'Permit? We're just trying to get to Varapalomas and the bastard of a taxi driver dumped us here.'

'That's because every resident on this island must have a permit to travel outside their locality, and he presumably didn't. Well, I have, so maybe your luck has changed. I'm going that way so I can take you.'

They jumped in the back his car where Arlene threw her arms around Stephen's neck and kissed him. This time though, he didn't extricate himself from her touch. Within the hour they were at the resort, cruising the front till they recognised their high-rise hotel. Here they found many worried people hugely relieved at the safe return of 'los perdidos'. Too late for supper, they strolled out along the beach with their rescuer and several of their coach party to a late bar. Again, they were last to leave.

Stopping on their way back to the hotel, they lay on the beach where Stephen was happy to receive Arlene's guided tour of the gold-stippled dome above. Then:

'Where is your bracelet?' she asked.

'This star is reborn,' he replied. 'He doesn't fear space anymore.'

Stephen took her hand.

'So where shall we venture out for lunch tomorrow?'

January 1st, 2021

Alix Edwards

'Grab me a beer!'
It's night. We cruise. Fireworks punctuate muggy air.

Countdown's over. Everywhere's shut. 'The drive-by!'
Mel's Steel Train. That tight-fisted bastard's bound to be
working.

We stop in a car park. The neon sign has no 'i.' 'Pass me the
spliff, Orlando.'
The sweet, heady weight of marijuana fills me with
optimism. 'So, what's your resolution, *paisa*?'
'To live!' I drop the six-pack on his lap.

But God has different plans.

Furze

Leusa Lloyd

Kissing is out of fashion
When the gorse is in blossom.
(Is that why I'm refused?)
I watch the little yellow lights that
Dance upon the pricking branches.

The flower that fire fuels:
For as it sets the furze aflame
The heat enacts a metamorphosis
So she may rise again,
For when she's just a heap of ashes
And you think that you broke her –
You are wrong –
For she rises thicker than before
And once again shines ochre,
And when winter comes, like an alabaster shroud,
She'll keep her emerald green and still be seen from all
around,
Against the wind she'll still stand proud.

Refuse me, then,
And set me again alight –
For I am built of furze and fury and flame:
        You'll never stop me burning bright.

Poplars

Angela Edwards

Five of them in the next garden and I wonder why they grow in a row, instead of by themselves – rippling and whispering in soft air, leaves turning and shining in the sun. Then waving and roaring in the wind as if the sea is coming. Climbing the fence and a branch arm comes to me, then a face with strings of leaves growing from its mouth, pulling me in with them to whisper forever.

Meeting

Morgan Fackrell

I am standing in a room, a darkened room with mood
    lighting,
Party lighting, or just dimmed to hide its undecorated state.
With my little gang of friends, who I have gathered, tended
And woven around me,
Dancing awkwardly to music set by our hosts who are
    absent.
It is a badly attended party, it is a little boring.
I will stay a while, invited by friends,
our hosts are busy in another part of the house,
perhaps there, it is less dull.
You told me later, you watched, as I spoke up over the music
Suggesting if it doesn't get any better, we'll go clubbing.
That was when you thought I was cool, but you used more
    words
Or you thought I was something else altogether.
I don't know how I'm sitting on the sofa next to you,
My usual – try to talk to the cute girl at a party thing –
    probably.
Friends are still dancing, looking over,
Did I bet them I could get you to come clubbing with us.
You tell me later you don't do clubbing, too noisy, you have
    sensitive hearing,
Or you don't like the music, or crowded places,
Whatever it was we didn't go clubbing.

We are talking and discover we find the same things funny,
You have such beautiful eyes, and a slight lisp,
Not quite a lisp, something about how your mouth moves,
Your smile, you are fascinating,
And we are talking, and I'm watching your lips move as it's
    noisy
Then we kiss, and we don't stop, I am transported away from
    this dim room
Away from thoughts of partying, friends, absent hosts
There is only this moment between us
My friends leave and I don't notice
The party is over and we are politely being asked to move on
We leave together and you come home with me.
And somewhere,
Between sitting down next to you and walking you home
I broke my heart, and shattered my faith in love ever
    working for me.
It took nine months to realise this.
On a sofa, at a housewarming party
My heart was doomed to break into shards of pain for the
    last time.
And two years later my soul broke when you left us all
    forever,
Leaving only echoes,
And memories,
Regret.

A journey to discover the aesthetic of women's pleasure through the *Kamasutra*

Sharha

At the age of nineteen, I was raped sixteen times over eighteen months by my boyfriend. I did not know what was desire, I did not know what was pleasure, and I did not even know what was consent. I just knew 'a female should compromise'. I was not in a committed relationship, I wanted to split up but I could not. One day during these eighteen months, he slapped me three times in the face, one by one. At the time, I did not realise that this boy was not for me, even though he was not a nice man. I started to question my sanity.

I was innocent and kept thinking that he was the only one who could give me love. However, I was wrong. Was that love, or just control and power over a woman? We broke up after eighteen months. Definitely it was the right decision, but I was disappointed because he made this decision after destroying my self-respect and my body. I wanted to split up first. I did not think I had the right to decide. I wish I had taken this decision.

Time passed, I was healing but I took another chance. I met someone else after four years. Initially, he made me feel important to him. Despite my scepticism, he gave me his time and support. I kept wondering, did I need him? I did not want to be in a relationship again but somehow I was involved. Every woman should be allowed to focus on herself first but I ignored myself, my pleasure, my consent, and my desire. I was only concerned about his feelings. However, there was something which I did not like, he kept saying 'Don't make it difficult. You should understand'. In the beginning, I wasn't bothered by these two sentences but I eventually felt suffocated. My life started to seem meaningless when I could not see his concern for me, an extremely manipulative tactic. I suffered from depression, anxiety, and panic attacks. A migraine also struck me.

My mistake in his eyes was to choose the United Kingdom for my research and my future. Did I make a mistake or did I have a right? This relationship ruined my mental health. I was about to commit suicide but I didn't break despite his emotional harassment. As an Indian woman, I was taught that 'women should compromise' while my research kept saying every day 'oh please, at this stage, don't do this, don't let him dominate you'. I realised that he was a psychopathic man. As a result of the abuse I gave up on this toxic man after six years. I listened to the voice of my research. The essence of love is not to control it.

I started to take therapies; my therapist told me I had given my power to him. Why did I do this? Perhaps women are not taught how to hold their power, or weak men need someone else's power to stay in the spotlight. Indeed, it seemed he was a coward due to his weakness, running away from complicated situations. It was apparent he was strong physically, but not internally. He didn't know how to face difficult situations, not just in a relationship but also in life. Throughout these six years, he never said 'sorry' once. Is it difficult to speak the word 'sorry' for a man, does it hurt their ego if they do? He enjoyed hurting me, kept smiling when he saw me with tears. He was confident that I could not leave him despite his emotional assault. I don't think these abusers are aware of emotional violence or, if they are, they simply ignore it. It highlights that they may be wrong which they feel they can't possibly be.

I still remember a big day in April 2018 when I found a book in the library of the University of Cambridge, related to pleasure and consent, *Redeeming the Kamasutra*[1] written by Wendy Doniger. She is an American Indologist who has worked a lot on the *Kamasutra*, including the translation of the *Kamasutra* in 2002. This is a book about women's pleasure and freedom, which was written by an Indian philosopher two thousand years ago. It fascinated me. As I started to read, the book gave me a powerful feeling. At that moment, I thought I had found my safeguard. The ethics of the *Kamasutra* define the art of living and I believe, the art of gender equality. Every woman should know about this art form. In September 2018, I reached Cardiff, ready to search for my freedom.

In 2019, I saw the campaign in Cardiff, 'This is not love. This is control', which emphasised that nobody has the right to be controlled by someone else. With more information and more confidence, I was able to finally end that damaging relationship and get my power back.

Researching women's empowerment made me aware that it is also a big issue in western cultures. These two men convinced me to challenge abusive masculinity through the *Kamasutra*, an ancient text which holds women's freedom at its centre.

I must say, my research saved me, Cardiff saved me. Now I am thirty-four years old, a single, independent woman, still actively researching my chosen subject, 'Freedom and gender equality through pleasure'.

What did I learn from these two episodes? Both men were

---

[1] Doniger, W. (2016). *Redeeming the Kamasutra*. Oxford University Press.

highly selfish, egotistic and always put their own desires first. I noticed that while physically I was there, mentally I was not, it was impossible for me to breathe in these relationships. My desire and my pleasure were not addressed, and certainly my consent was not asked for.

When we talk about pleasure or desire, I always observe, it connects to sexual pleasure. However, women can enjoy many other kinds of pleasure too. For example, fashion, dancing, singing, playing cards, reading, teaching, learning, writing, wearing and crafting jewellery, applying perfume, eating, cooking, gardening, travelling and so on. Sadly, fifteen years ago, I did not know about all these things.

The aesthetic of the ancient text talks about desire, consent, and importantly freedom which I did not have, or you could say I did not know about. In the same year 2018, Deepa Narayan articulated, it started with the early training of females by mothers[2]. Why is a little vagina taught by her mother to compromise and maintain silence? I accept that mothers were also taught by their mothers too, a culture passed from generation to generation, 'a compromise culture' or 'a silent culture'.

Why aren't more women breaking these cultural norms? I assume it is difficult to break stereotypes. Hence, I selected my research area to address this. I aimed to discover a contemporary and fresh feeling through the ancient writing, which seems to be a mystery to people these days. Violence is not tolerated in the *Kamasutra*. A storyteller, Seema Anand cited in 2018, 'the world desperately needs the Kamasutra'[3]. In the

---

[2] Narayana, Deepa (2018). *Chup: Breaking the Silence about India's Women*. Juggernaut.

[3] Anand, S. (2018). Available at:
<https://www.youthkiawaaz.com/2018/08/author-seema-anand-interview-on-why-the-world-needs-kama-sutra/>

third century, the author of the *Kamasutra* stated that the text was written to enliven the classical context with modern ideas and relate to human nature.

As acknowledged, the *Kamasutra* is a taboo subject in India. I had not heard about it until I started my research journey. In addition, contemporary audiences think it is an unruly and formidable context due to its religious aspects or the shame of eroticism. Importantly, the whole world thinks of it as a sex manual. In the contemporary market it is seen with the name of a condom brand or examined for sexual positions. It makes me annoyed, modern people are missing a royal and rich context from their own lives. They simply maintain the hierarchy of religious aspects made by older generations. They sweep it under the carpet due to their fear of discussing it openly.

My research tells me it is a sophisticated ancient text about human desire. It cannot destroy any religion. I have started to introduce myself as a Kamasutra Feminist. It seems like it belongs to me and indeed you can also look at it as my safeguard. The author of the *Kamasutra* wrote that every woman should read the *Kamasutra* and implement feminist principles in their lives.

Being a Kamasutra Feminist, I believe women's pleasure is paramount, not for compromising. It is a human right. When we talk about the aesthetics of this ancient writing, it defines the contours of pleasure, desire and love. It draws them passionately but they also remain invisible, an enigma of freedom. Doniger argued in 2016, 'Kamasutra is a feminist text'.

My investigation explores how women's pleasure is required for liberation and why this message is essential for contemporary people. In my research, I present Kamasutra

Feminism as written by Vatsyayana, author of the *Kamasutra* which is hidden. Nobody can see its feminist values. According to him, it has a significant impact on both men and women. The pleasure of women needs to be understood by men as well. Vatsyayana was also a man, a man of ancient times. An ancient man wrote a huge, strong book on women's pleasure, why do modern men not care about women's pleasure?

Social norms allow men more freedom than women, so nobody wants to talk about it. Women's pleasure or desire is not a big concern for men. They take it very easy, making jokes within their friends' circles. Women do not want to exploit their own sexuality in public, there is no safe place. I keep thinking every day about it and conclude that women are trained to follow decisions instead of making the decisions and this is not consent, I am sure.

Pleasure belongs to equality, equality belongs to women and women belong to society. Vatsyayana wrote, a woman's body is like a flower, very delicate, it needs to be treated very tenderly. He was an advocate of women's pleasure, as Doniger explained. The recognition of the female body is important for both women and men. The *Kamasutra* is not about how to seduce a man, it is about how seduction should be treated as the essence of life through human pleasure. Pleasure describes freedom both inside women and over women.

To find pleasure has been a distinct journey in my life. Women's pleasure is full of colour, very bright, joyful, very delicate and truly powerful. I can see that desire is an aspect of nature, a perfect feeling of creation, like the acting of senses, the voice of blowing air, the meandering pattern in the sea and the unseen stories of every woman. As a Kamasutra Feminist, I am investigating the hidden pleasure, which is weightless and priceless, everyone has, but they do not know.

Women have their own individual journeys towards hedonism. I did hurt, and I do not want to hurt again. The author of this ancient writing keeps warning each woman, you have the freedom to show your own desire, you have a voice to talk about it, you do not need permission from others, just enjoy it, because it is a soft beauty which every woman wears. It touches a woman's soul in a passionate way. We just need to catch it.

Surely, the *Kamasutra* is a guide of freedom for contemporary women. Freedom is just like a taste of pleasure, which I can feel, I can see. Being a woman and a researcher, I trust freedom transcends the meaning of our lives. I discover freedom, voice, pleasure and power over traditional norms. The *Kamasutra* belongs to women. I must say women belong to the *Kamasutra*.

Superstition

Nick Dunn

My question is this:

If I see two magpies,
but their number starts to change,
am I to meet a girl,
and then a boy,
find some silver
turning gold?

Will I see my sorrow
on feathered wings take flight?

Or is superstition folly?

If I walk beneath a ladder,
but quickly knock on wood,
or never break a mirror,
but cross upon the stairs,
will I simply be avoided
by Miss Fortune and Sir Prize?

The answer is:

I do not know.

Perhaps I never will.

But this I know for certain:

The solitary magpie
is rarely all alone,
nor is a pair eternal.

Sorrow is but fleeting
and sadly,
so is joy.
The one must be endured
that the other can be savoured.

Masterpiece

Jane King

He worked feverishly. There was a mood at night which inspired him and he was enraptured in the silence.

Well before sunrise it was complete. His wild energy had been captured magnificently. Theo, his brother, arrived with bread and cheese and he ate ravenously. The depth of the new work stopped speech.

They walked in the early morning light, Theo still awed. The starry night had been recorded by Vincent for posterity.

Ways in which a cortado can prompt existentialism no 19

Lesley James

Burgundy leather, almost flat, chisel-toed, zip-sided boots, shown off by ankle-grazing trousers. The old woman is thin, grey-haired, in dense black apart from the footwear. Her jacket fits well. Leather gloves buttoned past the wrist. And, barely visible, joy of joys: a small black velvet crescent hat, with tiny black feathers, hat-pinned ffs, to the back of her head. She avoids eye-contact, sitting upright. She fishes out a card – order of service? – from a glossy black handbag and sips a cortado.

A fanfare of howling… a primary school version of the arrival of the Queen of Sheba makes everyone look. A woman comes into the café, trailed by a screeching toddler dragging a toy dog on its side behind her.

The little girl howls like her dog has died. She cries big and wet, snot everywhere, snuffling in time to her steps. This has to be *the – endofthe – world.*

She looks like a child out of *Knitting Monthly* – complete with the pattern for a complicated granny-knit cardi. Or *Mother and Baby Magazine* – Perfect Summer Style for Your Child – braids close to the head, batik dress, hemline just above some pastel ankle socks.

But then the shoes.

Only a child would choose those shoes. Purple. Hologram-sparkly. Shoes to click twice and summon fairies. Shoes to be defiant. Shoes waiting to get this party started. Tears plop onto them.

Mum has seen it all before, but it's their turn in the queue and she needs to be heard.

> – *How many times? Mammy doesn't have to buy you something **every** time we go out.*

More howling; the girl's eyelashes plump with tears.

The barista, who has a toddler of his own, takes deep breaths. This child has real vocal abilities – think Minnie Ripperton, Monserrat Caballé, Mariah Carey. A dog outside starts to yowl. For a moment it's a freeze-frame with the volume turned up full.

The old lady gets up from her seat and steps towards the counter. Surprising and agile.

She addresses the child.

> – *My goodness, don't you look smart today.*

There's a gulp of wet silence. Before the girl can gather more sobbing momentum, the old lady carries on:

> – *What a pretty dress. And what amazing sandals. Are they your favourites?*

133

The little girl nods. Silence now. The whole place is silent.

- *I really can't see why you're crying. Just look at those pretty shoes!*

The child does as she's told.

- *Y'see, when we wear our best shoes, we don't ever need to cry.*

And before the child's mum can say a word, the burgundy boots are gone.

Any Questions?

Eryl Samuels

Why is Graham not answering any questions tonight? Is there something wrong with him? Something bothering him? I mean, if he can name the seven wonders of the ancient world, the eight American Ivy-league Universities, all nine of the Navagraha, – a simple starter for ten in a pub quiz shouldn't faze him, should it?

So why do his eyes seem so vacant and glazed? Why are there droplets of sweat glistening in the fatty crinkles of his brow? Has he taken something? When he scrunches his face up and grunts like a constipated pig trying to squeeze a hard stool through a huddle of raw haemorrhoids, can he really not remember the Mongolian capital?

And is there a reason he keeps disappearing into the lavatory? Surely the acknowledged 'King of Trivia' doesn't need to google the capital of Mongolia on his mobile, or to furtively check a diagram of the periodic table that he's stuffed down the back of the cistern in the cubicle, does he?

Or is something not quite right with Graham? Is there some secret that he's hiding from everyone, even his teammates? Some knowledge that not even he wishes to impart?

Have his teammates even noticed that he's behaving differently? Oddly? It doesn't look like it, does it? Does their indifference mean they don't care, or do they just not perceive these things? Is it how things are in *The Quizketeers*? Are there things you just don't say? Things you never ask?

What exactly is his relationship to the others? Are they friends? Or is it an allegiance borne out of a common pursuit? Do they like him or merely tolerate him? Was he made captain because of his leadership qualities, or because of his personality? Or is it just because he is the best quizzer?

When they are not competing, when they are sitting in the saloon of the Red Cow with half-drunk pints of pale ale on the tables in front of them, do they ever talk about other things? Does he ever ask about their lives? About their families? About their hopes and dreams and fears? Do they ever ask him about his?

Who exactly is Graham? He's attended these quiz nights faithfully, wearing the same knitted jumper for over fifteen years, but does anybody know much about him? The real Graham? The private Graham? Is he married, or does he live alone? Does he have any siblings? Children? A job? What about his surname? If the quizmaster were to ask these questions, how many in the pub would be able to answer correctly?

When, during the break, Graham goes to the bar to order a pint of the usual, does it bring him joy to explain to the lads on the pool table how snooker was invented by Sir Neville Chamberlain in India in 1875? And when they respond, does he really not notice their sarcasm? Will he carry on regardless to tell them how the other Neville Chamberlain once managed a sisal plantation in the Bahamas? And did they know what sisal was? Did they want him to tell them? Did they know it was a tropical plant and that the fibres of the plant were used to make rope and rugs and dartboards, like the one over there in the corner? When finally he turns away, is he aware of the sniggering and the gestures they make behind his back?

How does he perceive himself?

How do others perceive him?

Does he realise that there's a disparity in those perceptions?

Standing at the bar alone, what is he thinking about when the young barmaid pulls at the pump? Is it about the shape that her body makes in her dress, or is he thinking of the tattoo of inter-linked hearts upon her shoulder? Does he wish to plunge into the depths of her cleavage, or does he wish only to fill her with his knowledge? Is he overcome by a sudden urge to inform her of the origins of the word tattoo? Must he tell her that it's a Samoan word first encountered by Captain Cook on his voyages of discovery in the Pacific? Can he resist adding that the name of Cook's boat was the HMS Endeavour?

And does he ever wonder why the barmaid always has to move away to serve someone else every time he engages her in conversation? Why she always seems so busy, even when he is the only customer in the bar?

Is Graham a genius or a buffoon?

When he laughs at his own jokes, are other people laughing with him, or at him? Does it matter?

After all, what's wrong with gathering facts like others collect stamps or spot trains? What's wrong with pursuing knowledge and recall like it is the ultimate validation? Isn't it good to be clever? Isn't all bullying borne out of jealousy, to cover up their own inadequacies?

When people tell him he's made pedanticity into an art form, why shouldn't he tell them straight that there is no such word as pedanticity?

How about when Graham sits alone in his house at night? Does he ask himself questions? Not mundane factual questions that he knows the answers to, but big questions? Fundamental questions that not even Wikipedia can answer? Questions that can't be given simple answers because there are no right or wrong answers? Questions about when time began and where space ends? Questions that make you challenge your whole understanding of time and space? Does he dismiss these as stupid questions or does he unquestioningly accept what he's read with a shrug, that it's all to do with the metric governing the size and geometry of spacetime?

If there is no straightforward right or wrong answer, is it a bad question or a good question? Is grey the only alternative to black and white?

When, for instance, Graham looks at a painting, does he merely diagnose that it is by, let's say, Marc Chagall, before reciting a bullet-point biography of the artist and his work? Does his heart maintain a regular beat? Does he see anything more than an abstract confusion of figures floating on a canvas of colours? Or does he stare at the image the way a baboon will sometimes look at its reflection in a shard of broken metal? As if it recognises itself. As if, deep in its brain, synapses are flickering and connecting in cognitive conflict? Does something profound happen behind those glazy eyes? Is he somehow different after than before? Is he changed? Or will he return happily to scratching his balls and picking fleas from his hair, as if nothing remarkable has transpired?

And what about the music questions that he's so good at? Does he actually listen to any of the hundreds of CDs and records that are categorised alphabetically on the shelves around his living room? When he indexes them and types their details into his Excel spreadsheet, does he note a subjective view on their qualities? When he reads the entries in his Encyclopédia of hit singles and albums and memorises the year and the position in the chart and the name of the songwriter, does he recall a particular time and place? Are fragrances and feelings associated with these memories? Are there special songs that he dances to alone in his bedroom over and over again? Does he hold his pen to his mouth like a microphone and close his eyes as he sings along?

Is Graham happy or unhappy? Does he know what happiness means?

Is it true that he was once engaged to a pretty Ukrainian girl? If it is true, then did he love her? Did he tell her that he loved her? Did he scream out *Ulan Bator* at the height of love-making?

And what has become of her? Did she leave him, or did he leave her? When he hears the name Donetsk on the news these days, does he think about her? Her sweet smile? Her soft skin? The way she giggled every time he wore his Doctor Who pyjamas? Or does he simply recount that Donetsk is a city in the eastern Ukraine? That it used to be called Hughestown, after the Welsh founder of the city?

Does he sometimes lie alone in bed thinking of her with hot salty tears soaking into his pillow?

Or is it only the memory of his mother that has this effect?

If, after the quiz tonight, he were to walk into his mother's room rather than his own bedroom, will it have changed in the eighteen months since she went away? Would the same sheets still be on the bed? Are the ornaments and figurines arranged neatly on the dressing table, just as they always were? Are his mother's clothes still in the wardrobe? Does he run his fingers through the soft material and hold them to his nose, inhaling deeply? And occasionally try them on, the way he used to? Or has he thrown them all out and closed his mind to all that stuff, dismissed it as just a whim of teenage curiosity and experimentation?

How about the polaroid of a plump child on a beach at Porthcawl on the bedside table? Has that been removed? And the framed picture next to it of a gawky young man in a dinner jacket? The young man who stares out of the picture into a bright mysterious future with an almost natural smile?

When Graham stood in his bathroom last night and stared at himself in the cabinet mirror, was he the baboon again? When he saw the angry pink blotches sprouting like lichen on his neck, did he acknowledge that something was different, that something was not quite as it should be? Or did his own features metamorphose into a collection of strange shapes and angles like a cubist painting? Unable to make sense of what was in front of him, did he walk away and ignore the strange rash? The same way he had ignored all the other symptoms? The lumpy growth, the frequent and painful urination, the loss of appetite? The illogical splattering of scarlet around the rim of the bowl?

If, later tonight, while on his way back from the pub, a sharp pain should shoot through his chest causing him to bend double in agony and crumple to the ground, will the fact that he is able to name the American Ivy-league Universities provide a source of comfort to him? Will he think, when he is falling, that I've started, so I'll finish?

When his head cracks on the kerb, will a light go out, or will a light come on?

While lying on the ground watching the blood stream into the gutter, will he try to reason his situation logically or will he perceive how little he understands? How little he's ever understood?

How long will he lie there before someone comes? Before someone realises he's missing?

And afterwards, will anybody ask why no one heard him shouting? Why no one saw him falling?

Unnecessary Necessary

Ian McNaughton

An unnecessary necessary slab of torment and comfort,
making me feel guilty for the time I spend with her.
'Should I be feeling this way?' I ask.
'Yes,' she says.
She knows the answer to everything. Being 'smart,' I suppose
she would.

Black and bruised, cracked and hacked,
Indented in my life, hand and jeans.
I feel lost without her, shackled yet free to leave whenever I
want.
How did I ever manage without her, especially in my teens?

The keeper of all my memories and witness to private chat.
There used to be a silence between us but now she can talk
back.
Just to me, I hope although I hear spies can listen in,
as long as it's not my mother then I don't really care... I think.

A friend and foe, an enemy of my time and a tunnel of escape.
The demon who trolls through my input and shows me lands
far and warm,
She knows it's wet and cold outside.
She's seductive and clever and always on my side.

She's a part of my body now, my hand face and ears,
a bit haggard and aged, a phone battling to keep its head high.
Her time has come and gone, been replaced and outsmarted,
A new one I should buy.

My relationship is one that if for one moment I think I have
lost her forever,
I panic and get sad.
That's how much she means to me,
yet I loathe her for making me feel so needy and bad.

I dropped her once and spread the already webbed cracked
screen.
On my laptop, I searched for new models,
I'm not so stupid as to use my phone.
She would break her motherboard heart and would
purposely wipe her memory of me and that of her own.
She could live without me but not me without her.

We get along fine and if I did not have one,
I would be frowned upon by society.
I would end up having just real friends and not know the
time or day.
I would book zero-rated hotels and for train tickets too much
I would pay.
I'd miss my birthday and that of others. I would not know
how many times I am being liked.
I would not know if I should be building a nuclear fallout
shelter.

Ok, yes, I admit it, I love my phone and most importantly,
I can use it to see if I have spinach on my teeth
or a boogie on my nose.

I am

Martin Buckridge

*Inspired by the true tale of an unfortunate lady in France
wrongly declared dead.*

'I'm sorry, sir, I can't.'

'What? Why not? There's money there.'

'Yes there's money alright, quite a lot in fact, but the account's frozen. Steve Smith is dead.'

'What do you mean he's dead? I'm sitting here, talking to you.'

'I see you, sir, and we are having a conversation, but you are not *the* Steve Smith of 19 The Circus, you can't be. The system says he died two months ago, his estate is in probate and his account frozen. Could you possibly be another Steve Smith? It's not exactly an unusual name.'

'This is rubbish. Look at my driver's license. *I am* the Steve Smith and I live at that address. You've known me for twenty years. We used to play squash together. There's got to be a mistake.'

'No, sir, the system never makes mistakes. Look, this is a copy of the grant of probate and a letter from the executors. If you were *the* Steve Smith, I would be talking to a dead man and you, sir, are clearly alive.'

'Just a minute, there's no death certificate in your file. You can't decide Steve Smith is dead without that.'

'Yes that is rather strange, sir, but the absence of a death certificate does not in itself prove that a person has not died. I'm sure Alfred the Great didn't have a death certificate.'

'What? What's Alfred the Great got to do with it?'

'He's dead, sir… no doubt about it.'

'This is a nightmare, last week my employer stopped my salary despite me sitting in the office at the time. The week before I had to prevent someone from fixing For Sale signs outside my house. And now, I can't even withdraw money from my own bank account. How can I prove to you that I am Steve Smith, owner of that bank account and all the money you're holding on to?'

'I think you'll have to prove to the system that you didn't die.'

'Ok, what's the procedure for doing that?'

'There isn't one…'

'Wait, let me guess… because the system never makes mistakes.'

'That's correct, sir.'

'Right, that does it … stick 'em up!'

'Be careful with that gun, sir. You'll never get away with this. You're on CCTV, your fingerprints everywhere and I make a very good witness.'

'Ah! That's where you're wrong. I can do anything I like. The police can't arrest a dead man and he can't be prosecuted… Now, open the safe.'

Is this a Conflagration?

Alexander Winter

Is it a match
behind that glint in your eye
the first spark hinting combustion
or just a trick of the light?
A trick of the lie
I'm telling myself.

Are you thinking what I'm thinking?
Are you grinning why I'm grinning?

Is it the wine?
Why your white cheeks glow with that rosé flush?
Why your front teeth go to test your bottom lip?

Are you staring why I'm staring?

Are you a bonfire in Midwinter
to be watched from the forest's edge?
where only the faintest breath of heat
can reach my parted lips?
Are you burning why I'm burning?

Am I
the charcoal and the kindling
edging toward an open flame?
Or are you pausing why I'm pausing?

When Your Child has a Child

Suzanne Shepherd

When your child has a child, it's a dream come true,
To love an extension, who's an extension of you.
You see in their face, your nose, or small trace,
Of you as a child, and your child in his face,
A third generation of your family's genes,
A beautiful baby full of hope and of dreams,
There's nothing quite like becoming a nan,
I feel overjoyed looking at my little man.

Haunted Blue

Patty Papageorgiou

She'd missed the ocean most of all.

No, that's a *lie*. Above all she misses her. But the ocean… the ocean is a close second.

Her greatest love and her worst enemy.

She stands on the shore, her long fins tucked under one arm. Sea froth licks her toes and they sink further into the wet sand. She breathes in the warm, salty air.

It's well past mid-day, the sun making its downward pass of the sky. The afternoon is now bathed in a more tolerable heat, luring people out of air-conditioned sanctums. Office workers, clocked out early, sipping iced coffees on beach loungers. Families with picnics spread on towels, children blowing sand off sandwiches. Here and there couples nuzzle each other under the privacy of low-hanging umbrellas.

There's splashing near her. A boy chases his little sister with a bucket of seawater. She runs from him giggling and stumbling.

Why am I here?

She watches the children play and remembers her giggle, like the sound of a thousand wind chimes. The way her grin would light up her little face – like the sun itself lived in her eyes. Her jet-black hair, matted with salt and sand. Melted ice cream drying on her chin.

They had built sandcastles here. Spent hours looking for shells and pebbles to decorate them. They snorkelled around the rocks, looking for urchin shells to put on the towers. They'd count to three – *one-two-three* – take a deep breath and dive together, gliding hand in hand above the rocks, hunting for their treasures.

Her little mermaid. She was fearless in the water.

She turns and walks along the shore. Lazy waves erase the foot-shaped puddles she leaves behind.

This is the place she visits in the twilight between dreaming and waking.

Am I really here? Or was that another lifetime?

She gazes at the horizon and images of her own childhood come unbidden; dolphins following her dad's boat, her hand reaching out to stroke the glistening bodies, the boy who took her up the cliff on his bike to watch the sunset. Starfish everywhere, on the beach and on the seabed, a night sky underwater.

She used to dive deeper and longer than any of her friends, waiting for shy sea creatures to come out of their hiding holes.

It all looks different now. Cafeterias. Cigarette butts in the sand. Too many people. She watches them and idly wonders if they were here five years ago. If they'd heard her screams, or read the papers afterwards. If they shook their heads sadly at the headlines.

Maybe I'm the only one who remembers.

Her mother's last words to her ring in her head. *You shouldn't have let her out of your sight.* Last words because she'd hung up the phone there and then and never spoke to her again. Not even after her husband and herself packed up their guilt and grief and took the remains of their lives somewhere else.

They made a new home somewhere far away, where rain falls intolerably and dragons breathe over mountains. A green paradise with no haunted blue waters to gaze into.

The sun is hot on her shoulders. She takes a few steps into the undulating sea. Despite the heat, the water feels cold around her midriff. She splashes handfuls on her skin to acclimatise. Then, with a committed, deep breath, plunges.

The shock of the temperature change courses through her body as quickly as it subsides. She resurfaces with her head tipped back, allowing the water to slick her hair away from her eyes. She sluices it off her face and licks the saltiness on her lips.

Tastes like home.

She lies on her back, floating with a fin under each arm, and shuts her eyes against the glare of the sun. The gentle waves rock her.

How she missed this free-floating sensation. This amniotic lullaby.

Home is where the heart is, they say.

Time heals. That's another thing they say.

Time passes. Healing is another matter.

Her husband wanted another baby. It would help, he said. To move on. But she couldn't. She couldn't tell him about the resentment she suddenly felt towards children. The audacity of their existence. She didn't *want* to feel that way. But something had broken inside her, something she couldn't fix.

He immersed himself in work. He left early and stayed late. He took business trips. She didn't begrudge him that. He dealt with grief in his way and she loved him enough to allow him that.

She knew he wasn't alone on those trips. But she didn't mind that either. If he had found someone who could mend his heart, that was ok.

But the mountains around their new home hemmed her in. She missed the unobstructed seascapes of her childhood, the blue horizon with its imperceptible curve, marking the shape of the planet.

That visceral pull of the ocean.

She opens her eyes and tips herself upright, treading water. One at a time, she slips her fins on and kicks, gently drifting further out, away from the noisy bathers. In one fluid movement she inhales, turns and slides into the wet, deep silence.

She is overcome by a sense of serenity almost forgotten. Here, she is her own goddess, unconnected to the world yet connected to everything. Here, she is a weightless spirit, dancing in blades of sunlight that try to pierce the abyss.

Down here, the weight of the ocean is a warm hug wrapped around her soul.

Home.

In her dreams she's often underwater, breathing, belonging. She could stay in those dreams forever.

With a flick of her hips, she glides towards a rock formation. Hermit crabs scuttle on the sand, others burrow in to hide. She picks shells out of crevices, examines them, puts them back gently.

She suppresses the slow burn now rising in her lungs. There's time yet. Hand over hand she slowly pulls herself along the rocks, peering into the spaces between them. If she stays still, curious fish will poke their heads out to say hello.

She follows a little blue-and-yellow wrasse as it pecks through patches of moss.

Her lungs remind her again that it's time to resurface. A fresh breath and she can come back to it.

She's about to head up when she glimpses a flash of brilliant green behind a rock. She pushes down the urge to breathe and swims towards it.

And then she sees her.

An emerald tail, a jet-black trail of hair. Striped urchin domes clutched in small hands.

Her heart leaps. The surface beckons still but the sea holds her tight.

The little mermaid's eyes meet hers. Her lips part in a smile with a tinkling of wind chimes.

I see you.

The surface calls for her to return for air.

No. Not yet.

She grabs hold of the rock, anchoring herself as the smiling girl glides towards her. Light dances around the edges of her vision.

With a halo of black hair she floats before her, eyes full of sunlight.

Her lungs burn, but the mermaid holds out her hand.

Come.

Her own hand reaches out and touches the small fingers. A sudden calm enfolds her and her heart sings with joy as she pulls her into an embrace.

Breathe.

The Public Path

AH Creed

Hey, riverbank sandwich-bag. Did you slip silently from a
water-watcher's pocket?

Hey, bluebell-snapping beanie. Were you thrown by a
Mummy's-on-her-mobile toddler?

Hey, oak-rooted Stella cans. Are you the hand-crushed
discards of a home from no home?

Hey, memorial bench. Were your slat-stuffed scratch card and
blackened tin foil someone's twin Horsemen of Hope and
Despair?

Hey, fence-jumping flatulence of late-for-work cars. You are
invisible, but are you the most denaturing litter of all?

Just a Mug

Nejra Ćehić

I chose a mug for thirty-five pounds.
They called it expensive,
They called it extravagant,
My mug for thirty-five pounds.

My hands circle ceramic, sensing the surface etched with my
    zodiac sign,
Hand-made
Hand-painted
In pink, purple, gold and teal – a steal,
My mug for thirty-five pounds.

It replaces a cupboard full of mugs not chosen.

I fill my mug, then I fill myself.
My mug sits beside me as I create.
My mug holds inspiration.

But it's just a mug.
I could use someone else's,
That'll do just fine.

Except
This time I choose what I hold

And what holds me,
The source from which my ideas flow, replenishing them

From a framework so familiar
I didn't pay attention to whose it was,
From whom it was inherited, borrowed, accepted
Until I chose my mug for thirty-five pounds

Owner's Guide to The Human Body

Jeff Robson

A — Armpit… Many people think this is perhaps the smelliest and sweatiest thing about their bodies. Little do they know.

B — Bottom… Used mostly for sitting on in front of the TV set, only raising occasionally to relieve gaseous pressure or to go to the kitchen to make a cup of tea.

C — Chest… Or the top half of the trunk directly below the head. Mostly flat unless you happen to be female. Moves in, out and upwards when inhaling and exhaling.

D — Digits… Better known as fingers. Mostly used for signalling your unhappiness to other drivers. Alternate uses: cleaning nasal passages or moving food in the direction of the mouthparts. See M.

E — Ears… Funny looking cartilaginous protuberances that stick out from the side of the head, almost but not quite in line with the eyes. Mostly ugly. Used to enhance sound entering the ear canal. Also good for hanging things from. See H.

F — Feet… Make note: here should be two of similar size. Without feet the stumps of the legs would be difficult to balance on. They take the shape of a right angle from the base of the leg. Feet also have fingers, designated the name toes, five on each. They are useless at grabbing and holding things.

G—Gut... This part is always on the inside of the body. Just as well as it would make you look stupid if it was hanging out dragging on the ground. The gut consists of a long tube all coiled up. Do not attempt to visualise it by opening up the belly to take a look. This part does the job of assimilating the food you eat, turning it into energy. For waste products refer to B.

H—Hearing... When sound enters the ear canal via the outer cartilaginous sticking out bits at the side of the head (see E) the noise makes a membrane vibrate, this in turn makes three small bones shake and dance to the music. A signal from these enters the brain to be interpreted as ABBA on a bad day.

I—Intestines... Coiled tight within body (see G). You have miles of it. Mostly not needed. Serious drinkers barely ever fill it with food.

J—Jugular... Basically for blood supply to and from the brain. In some cases not enough blood, leading to abstract behaviour from criminals and those who hate mathematics.

K—Knee... Articulated joint halfway between the bottom and the ground. The knee allows a swinging movement of the lower leg. On occasion becomes painful especially when grovelling for a raise from your boss.

L—Legs... Continuation of the bottom (see B) where they attach at the top then reach all the way to the ground via the feet (see F). Muscle bound and lumpy, the legs support the weight of the body. Some more than others.

M — Mucus... (see N) Also known as snot, bi-product of a sneeze as it leaves the nostrils at two hundred miles an hour. Anybody within range will share this sticky semi-liquid with you. Best to sneeze into a tissue. Children are known to have the equivalent of candles of snot running from these two holes in their faces.

N — Nose... Contains the nostrils. Responsible for discharging large amounts of mucus (see M). Other uses... On occasion used for breathing when mouth is shut or chewing food. Smelling, the nose itself does not smell as such but instead has a system inside that can determine if underwear can be worn again for the third time that week. Quite useful. The nose cannot be missed as it stands rampant in the middle of the face.

O — Organs... Neatly tucked inside the body cavity, each having a specific function. Heart, Kidneys, Liver, Spleen and Brain etc. Medical science has made great strides in being able to replace each organ as it fails due to illness or old age. Warning... Do not attempt to replace these organs yourself even if you have a suitable donor. Murder is still considered a crime even in these times. Best to leave it to the professionals, Mr Burke and Mr Hare.

P — Penis... Usually male only. Connected to the bladder for urination. Lesser-known use is for procreation/fun. Chance would be a fine thing. Note... not to be played with.

Q — Quiff... Relating to hair. Human hair is a left over from our evolutionary past. It tends to grow thickest on top of the head.

Unless that is you are male of a certain age and are a stud. If classified as a stud then your head hair will disappear. The female of the species does not tend to lose head hair due to a female hormone that the male body does not have access to. Women however are not proud of hair on other parts of their bodies. They make a great deal out of removing as much of it as they can, usually painfully.

R—Ribs... Bony structures set in the chest area. They keep things inside from falling out and protect them from damage from outside. Muscles between the ribs, the intercostals, help the ribs to contract and expand when breathing in and out (see C). Do not try to pull on these ribs in an attempt to force them apart. When it comes time for your heart bypass the nice surgeon will do that for you.

S—Shin... Relating to part of the leg (see L) below the knee (see K). Made up of two bones attached at the knee and the heel slightly above the foot (see F). Prone to fracture especially if a professional footballer known as 'Chopper' kicks when trying to take the ball from you.

T—Tongue... Many a harsh word has been blamed on this organ or an answer has been lost on its tip. The only muscle in the body that is only connected at one end. Known mostly for being capable of tasting a range of different flavours. Strange because when the nose (see N) is blocked with mucus (see M) the tongue loses this ability.

U—Umbilical... Mainly refers to how babies absail inside their mother's womb when climbing from one side to the other. It helps prevent them from falling out.

V – Vagina... Mostly female. Referring to lady bits that to most men are completely unfathomable.

W – Womb... Relating to internal parts of the female body. Restricted to the production of children. Can be fooled into thinking it is already full. Keep taking the tablets.

X – XX XY... Chromosomes. Depending on whether you are male or female you will have a selection. On occasion there can be a mixture that can lead to a decided variation between male and female. When this happens life can be challenging. But fun.

Y – Yellowing... Mostly of eyes when jaundiced. Eyes are at their most colourful when red and yellow, standard when intoxicated and jaundiced at the same time.

Z – Zoological... The human being has been found to be descended from the Great Apes. Coming down from the trees was probably not one of mankind's best moves. However, we did. In the millions of years since this momentous occasion the human race has invented such things as ... computer games, pollution and world war. It would have been safer to have stayed in the trees.

She Said, I Said

Paul Jauregui

She said there was something she wanted to do. Together. Couldn't do it alone.

I said no. Didn't fancy that.

She said if I loved her I'd do it. With her. For her. Said one of her friends and her partner did it. Would I prefer she found someone else to do it with? And what about that... 'thing'... she does with me because I like it even though she hates it.

I said alright. We could try it Saturday night.

She loved it.

I didn't.

She insisted we do it again the following night. Loved it even more.

I didn't.

So every weekend she did... 'the thing'... I liked, and I did... 'the thing'... she liked.

Twice.

She told her friends what we did. They were jealous, because their partners refused to do it with them. For them. She said I should encourage the other husbands, boyfriends, partners, significant others, wives, girlfriends to do the... 'thing'.

I said that would sound very odd. How was I supposed to know their partners wanted... that? It could get physical.

Next time we were all together, she told everyone what I did with her. For her. The others laughed, but soon they were all doing it. Had no choice. Well, I was doing it.

So now we do this… 'thing'… for her, every weekend, even though she's stopped doing the other… 'thing'… for me.

And twice every week, together, we watch *Strictly*. And I watch *Doctor Who* alone.

Burial Rites

Sarah Mayo

I'd scatter crystals,
incant to the tendrils
of the earth,
implore the soil
to absorb
the decay.

I'd kiss the sky
and serenade the sun,
so the ground
would give birth
to roots ready
to bloom

into a cherry blossom tree,
bearing testimony
that in the right season
flowers thrive.

Cruyff's Last Match for the Bluebirds in '75

Eryl Samuel

It's the final. Cardiff are beating Liverpool, two-nil. Cruyff is on a hat-trick. We're on the verge of glory. I look on in horror as Lucy leaps onto the pitch and squats in the goalmouth. Again!

'Mum!' I cry, but it's too late. There is a sharp snap. I know instantly it's Cruyff that's down.

The plastic fans gawp blankly at the cat as she rolls on her side, swishing her tail over Kevin Keegan.

Music in their Hands

Sara Hayes

Haydn Jones was born into a musical family. His father Simon was a tenor, specialising in oratorio, his mother Frances, a euphonium player. He was immersed in the sound-world of nineteenth-century Vienna from the first beat of his heart. Trills and crescendos softened his cries; he was washed with bars of sliding glissandos, and Simon's arias tucked him up at night.

The family was regularly on the move: Europe, the US, China, Patagonia. He saw plenty of Customs but little culture, moving as he did between plane and hotel, hotel and plane.

One rainy morning in New York, he was scribbling circles on a hotel notepad with a shiny black pen, when he said,

'Mummy, Daddy, can we stay in today?'

'No, sweetie,' said Frances.

'But I just want to watch telly!'

Frances and Simon looked at each other.

'Please?'

'You'll feel better with food in your tummy.'

At breakfast they sat at their usual table with its fresh red carnation in a glass vase. Haydn, sullen, pulled the flower apart, scattering petals around his chair. The bald stalk smelt like apple flesh but tasted bitter. He mixed salty bacon into his sugary porridge and made slurping noises as he ate.

'This is amazing!' he said, crunching rind, porridge escaping his mouth.

'Shh!' hissed Frances.

'Try it,' he demanded, holding a dripping spoon to Frances's mouth. 'Try it!'

'Right! Out!' erupted Simon.

Back in the apartment Simon and Frances paced, avoiding eye contact. Haydn sat on the bed eating chocolate from the mini-fridge.

Next morning Haydn was playing traffic jams, still in his pyjamas.

'Haydn, how old are you?'

It hurt that Daddy didn't remember.

'Five.'

'You're a big boy now.'

Haydn was wary of what was coming. He stood up, walked to Frances, and leant against her.

'We've put your name down for school,' said Frances, stroking his curly brown fringe into a side parting.

'Oh!'

Simon said, 'You'll start after Easter.'

'Do you really mean it?' Haydn asked. Having spent so long with adults, he was desperate to be with other children.

School was complex at first, he had to read eyes, body shapes and voice tones to understand unspoken meanings but he was a quick learner and, having been lonely for so long, a good friend.

As his parents suspected, school found Haydn talented on any instrument he picked up, a competent piano player and particularly enthusiastic on percussion. In Sixth Form he was Head Boy and sang with excellent diction in a quartet. He left school with a quintuplet of top marks and ringing references.

Haydn was unsure what to study in Uni so he took a year out. The answer came at the Last Night of the Welsh Proms, while watching exuberant conductor, Owain, who swished on stage in black tails with satin Welsh flag waistcoat.

'Mum, Dad, I've got something to tell you,' he declared that evening.

Frances and Simon raised eyebrows in unison and braced themselves for some big disclosure.

'I've decided to become,' and he raised his hands, '… a conductor.'

Simon coughed.

'That's… a surprise,' he said.

'Sounds exciting, darling,' said Frances, with little enthusiasm. She knew the struggles of a musician's life.

'Intriguing!!' said Simon.

'I'm going to set up a community choir, open to all, no auditions.'

'And how will you pay your way?' asked Simon.

'I'll teach piano, play at weddings. It'll be fine.'

That didn't give them the assurance they were looking for.

'Living here?'

Haydn heard a tremble in Frances's voice.

'I'll pay for my food if that's what you want.'

'We just want you to be happy,' she replied.

Haydn's bright posters resonated with the public, the turnout was good. As he hovered by the door, greeting newcomers, he was pleased to see a mix in ages, languages and genders. He called everyone together.

'Welcome to the first session of "Capital Chords", Cardiff's newest choir. My name is Haydn and I'm excited to be working with you all. Can't wait to get started. But first, give yourselves a clap for turning up.'

As the noise was trailing off Haydn saw some hand movements directed at him by one of the women at the front.

'Excuse me?' he said.

'She says you look young,' said a woman standing next to her.

'What?'

'You know, to be a choir leader. She expected an older person… she's saying, "not a schoolchild!"'

The room fell silent.

'I see. And what is your name?'

'Sonia. This is Vicki … and Andrew,' she said, pointing from one to the other. 'I can hear a little so I sign for them.'

'Thank you, and thank you Vicki,' he said, 'for your … compliment. Are you always this forthright?'

Vicki started signing again.

'She says yes, and she can lip read so you can't fool her.'

'Hell's bells, Vicki, you're a real Welsh dragon!'

Vicki signed back, with narrowed eyes,

'I breathe flames when I'm angry,' voiced Sonia, 'and mind your language.'

Haydn pretended to write in his notebook, to laughter:

'If Vicki upset, check fire extinguisher.'

Niceties over, he arranged them in a crescent, two-deep with Sonia, Vicki and Andrew in the front, so they could see him at the keyboard.

After the warm-up they sang nursery rhymes, changing words so they became even more ridiculous. But Haydn found it hard leading like this. He couldn't bring them in crisply.

'Can anyone play keyboard?'

After a pause a lanky young man with brown hair in a bun stepped forward.

'I… I can give it a go,' he said.

'Excellent, what is your name?'

'Gwyn.'

Timid Gwyn played brilliantly and from there, everything fell into place.

Sessions were fun and piece by piece, Haydn and Gwyn built up the repertoire. There were no scores, just the choir, learning and working together. Haydn appreciated how the three signers brought a visual dimension to the choir; their movements, fused with the dynamics of the music, heightened the emotional impact. Even the signers' faces were full of expression, the agonies and the ecstasies. But if they couldn't hear, why join a choir? He asked them at the end of one rehearsal.

'Can't you tell?' signed Andrew.

'How do we look?' asked Vicky.

'As though you are enjoying yourselves. You are always in time and you know the words…'

'We feel the beat through the floor and we follow you. We enjoy bringing rhythm in the signs to the lovely words,' said Sonia.

'Well, I'm glad you've joined us. If you need anything, or have any musical requests, let me know,' said Haydn.

After months of singing together, Haydn suggested the choir should start performing.

'What would we sing?'

'What would we wear?'

'Can our families come to see us?'

So yes, they agreed and started rehearsing. Haydn booked them into a charity slot in the Atrium on Level Three, St David's Hall one lunchtime.

Members suggested songs and Glyn played them from his phone, then they voted. The overwhelming favourite was 'Panis Angelicus' by Cesar Franck because they all wanted to sound like that.

'Good choice,' said Haydn. 'Bread from the angels. We'll win everyone over singing this. Remember, it's a big space we're filling, you need to sing out.'

Then the COVID-19 pandemic hit and swept everything away in a wave of face-covering litter, yellow and black sticky tape and society in shut-down.

St David's Hall was closed, indoor gatherings stopped and worst of all, singing was banned.

Simon, Frances and Haydn hated being stuck at home with no work. There were occasional socially-distanced commissions behind Perspex screens in recording studios but no live performances.

Within weeks they worked out the practicalities of video calls and slowly, tuition classes picked up for all three.

Haydn emailed his Chords members.

'With no end to lockdown in sight, shall we try rehearsals on-line? If interested, I'll set up a meeting and send joining instructions.'

'Yes please.'

'I'm not sure how to do it but I'll give it a go.'

'I'm going to give this a miss thanks. Spend all day on-line for work as it is.'

And so the e-sessions started. They would open with banter and then all but Haydn would mute for the warm-up and rehearsal. Numbers were good week after week so he had one more question for them.

'Hi Chords, fancy recording our piece? For our website? Discuss next sesh.'

With promise of support, he persuaded the choir to try. He emailed the instrumental track to each member, with instructions on how to video themselves singing while listening to the backing track on headphones. Several weeks later, with prompting, the tracks were in. He emailed round,

'Looking forward to playing you our first video.'

Then he checked the submissions, one at a time before trying to mix the audio tracks and sync them with the visuals. Confusing. The first one he listened to, smiley face, bright eyes, he could even lip read the words, but there was no audio. Technical error? Second one, same thing. The third, from Gwyn, was beautiful. His voice was clear, sensuous, like a rivulet flowing over pebbles.

'Give him a solo when we are back, he's a real find,' thought Haydn.

Then the fourth, silent.

The fifth was from Sonia, Vicki and Andrew. They had obviously practised, they signed perfectly together.

'I'll put them in the middle of the screen, with a larger tile,' thought Haydn, already building the video in his mind.

There were plenty more videos but only a few audio files.

'Mum, Dad, please can you help me?' he asked next morning.

At the next on-line session Haydn looked at anxious faces in the little squares.

'Let's call this the warm-up video,' he said as he clicked the start arrow.

It was better than it might have been. Gwyn's voice soared over the small number of less penetrating voices. The three signers were brilliant, moving fluently with the spirit of the words. The backing track held everything together but it was, if Haydn was honest, a touch comical.

When the video stopped, there was silence.

A young woman unmuted herself.

'I'm sorry, I tried singing but I couldn't get it right. So I mimed.'

'Yeh, me too. I sounded awful on the recording.'

'Sorry Haydn. We've let you down.'

'No, no you haven't. Not at all. What you've done is placed the spotlight on our new stars, firstly, Gwyn, who shared his grace so generously with us all. Gwyn, I played your file to my dad, Simon Jones.'

Gwyn put his hand over his mouth with surprise.

'Dad's offered to give you free lessons until you can get your own gigs, and access a recording studio, after which you will undoubtedly start selling records, earning your own fan base and all that follows, if you would like that.'

Gwyn grimaced a frightened face that turned into a grin.

The whole screen erupted with pairs of little clapping yellow hands in the top left-hand corner of the tiles.

'Secondly, the signers. Sonia, Vicki, Andrew, congratulations, you looked like the angels themselves. You belong centre-stage, the choir can wrap around you. Perhaps you can teach us to sign the song too.'

More yellow clapping hands appeared and the three pretended to bow.

'So, team, that was a trial run. I know you can do this. Have faith in yourselves. Don't worry if you go wrong, don't we all? I can cover over anything if there are enough of you singing. My parents and I have recorded four-part files for you. I'll send them round. You can choose which to sing with, whichever suits your voice best. Let rip, sing out and enjoy. No more miming. From now on, we are Capital Chords, singing and signing is what we do. We do nothing for appearance, we perform!'

Their video went viral. You can see it on-line, with Sonia, Vicki and Andrew moving as one, Gwyn standing tall, framed by lush brown hair, and Haydn leading them, baton dancing in his hand.

And, after lockdown, they sang and signed in a late-night event at the Welsh Proms, on Level 3 in front of the Stuttgart Window, when bread of heaven rained down again on the promenaders and revellers of St David's Hall.

Homophoneity

Saoirse Anton

Talking on the phone
the give us a buzz known life long
until a different sing-song
at the other end can't comprehend yours

But in the then, the here, the when,
lilts will always bend to mend
gaps in understanding.
It's a human thing
to story tell
how are you
well
across linguistic lines.

These accented attempts are mines
of humanity pure
where your words
stumble to a spark between
two new friends.

Like trees to thrive we bend
in a breeze of speech.

But, hold fast against the reach
of Homophoneity.

It doesn't sound like you or me
but a machine measured stilted
Alexa-lexicography.
Where a glottal stops you getting through
the questions on the phone
and kids don't talk like Mam or Dad
but parrot Google home.

It's a concrete voice.
Its tongue won't bend.
Its tone won't reach or sway.
There's no chance to say in different ways
to bridge the gaps, explore or play.

In homophonic monotone
there are no nonsense poems
no chance to roam
with spontaneity
And make up the words
you want to say,
like Homophoneity.

Seasons of Love and Haiku

Paul Jauregui

where are you?
deep within your heart
where am I?

as you join with me
carve footprints in my being
my life finds meaning

your warmth now
so deep and knowing
I am yours

as hearts awaken
your eyes light my existence
your season takes me

Zen and the Art of
the Complete Angler

Stephen Pritchard

I began to see him, the angler, on my morning walk. Always in the same spot, at the edge of the pond, where a gap in the bulrushes allowed him to cast his line. It was a small pond, I'd dug it myself, for the cattle to drink from. When this field had been part of a family farm; my family; my farm.

One day I left the footpath and went and stood near him. I watched his red-tipped float swaying in the water. 'You've got a good day for it,' I said chattily. He seemed to come back from a long way away before he looked up at me. He had one of those round, smooth faces that defy categorisation. He might have been thirty. He might have been sixty. Possibly Asian. Possibly Caucasian. He didn't speak, just smiled and nodded. I wondered if he'd understood me.

'If you don't mind my saying,' I continued, gently, not wishing to upset him, 'there are no fish in this pond. There never have been.'

He nodded slowly, three times, before saying, patiently, as if I were the one who didn't understand, 'Of course. That is why I have no hook on the end of my line.'

Tea For Three

Jacqueline L Swift

'It must be time now,' whined Maggie. 'The big hand's gone round loads of times.'

'A hundred times,' agreed Tommy. 'A thousand times.'

'A thousand, million times.'

'A million, million times.'

Twins Tommy and Maggie grinned at their big brother Malcolm, who smiled back at them. His siblings' faces glowed in the flickering candlelight, a light which failed to reach the corners of the dark damp cellar.

'We have to wait, remember what Mummy said?' Malcolm looked at his six-year-old brother and sister. Double the trouble, Grandma used to say, but double the love Grandpa would chip in.

Malcolm remembered the photographs of his parents as children amongst a plethora of other family photos sat on top of the mantlepiece above the drawing room fireplace. They had been his mother's pride and joy, a window into the past she'd always said. And how Maggie looked just like their mother did at her age and Tommy was the double of their father. Blonde with blue eyes. Enormous blue eyes. Not like him. Nothing like him. Malcolm often wondered whom he took after, with his jet-black hair. Perhaps his mother's parents, the grandparents he never knew. He adjusted the spectacles on his nose and shivered. A chill ran through him, and not because of the cold. He opened the envelope and read the contents again.

My dearest Malcolm,
Remember what we discussed? Tea at five. No earlier. Promise me.
Remember. At five.
Love you all, Mummy XXX

'Can I see?' Maggie shuffled next to her older brother. She was dressed in her best frock; their mother had insisted they dress to impress for their tea below stairs. Tommy wore his one and only suit, only ever worn for special occasions. And he, Malcolm, had donned what had once been his father's wedding suit, taken in for him by Grandma.

He gave Maggie the note.

'Three kisses.' Maggie smiled.

'One for each of us.' Malcolm drew in a deep breath, determined to keep his expression as neutral as possible.

'Look Tommy, one for you, too.'

Tommy screwed up his face at the mere thought of a kiss.

Malcolm tried to smile at this innocent reaction but could not. What he wouldn't give for a bone-crushing hug from Grandma or a tender goodnight kiss on the forehead from Father as he finished reading them a bedtime story.

The twins could not remember their father. He'd left just after the twins were born. Malcolm was eight years old and could remember crying for weeks.

'You're the man of the house now, Malcolm,' Mother had said.

There were times when he didn't want to be man of the house. He wanted to play outside with his friends, but when his grandparents left, at the time he didn't know why, only now he was older did he understand the reason. He had to man-up, as Grandpa used to say to Father, so he did.

And here he was fourteen, and in charge of his brother and

sister yet again, but this time it was different. This time it was important, more important than anything his mother had ever asked him to do in the past. He had lost count of how many times he had 'baby-sat' his siblings, while his mother attended her vital meetings. He didn't mind at all, he loved Maggie and Tommy and tried very much to be their big brother as well as their missing father. He never let Mother down.

'Malcy, can we have a drink now?' Tommy approached the picnic basket and lifted the lid.

'No.' Malcolm dashed across the floor. 'Not yet. We have to wait.' He slammed the lid down.

'But we've been waiting a long time. Mummy never makes us wait a long time.' Maggie pouted. She looked toward the stepladder, lying on its side. 'I want to go up; I don't like it down here.'

'Neither do I.' Tommy joined in.

'It's too dark, why can't you light the oil lamp? Mummy always lights the oil lamp.'

'You know why. Because of the smell.' Malcolm looked at the twins who were on the verge of tears.

'I want Mummy,' Maggie sobbed.

'I want Mummy, too.' Tommy's bottom lip quivered.

'Hey, remember we have to be like mice.' Malcolm attempted to keep his voice light as he wiggled his fingers by his cheeks, pretending they were whiskers. 'You know, quiet and invisible.'

'From the bad people?' Maggie wiped her eyes.

Malcolm stared at her, a pulse thrummed above his eye as he searched for an answer.

'Did they take Daddy?' Tommy looked at his older brother. 'William next door said that Daddy was like a cockroach and had to be exter… mined or something.'

'William next door's a fool.' Malcolm's voice shook. 'You've been told not to speak to him, haven't you?'

'He said we're all like insects crawling in the dirt, and have to be stomped on.'

Malcolm placed his hands on Tommy's shoulders and closed his eyes. His chest tightened, and nausea threatened.

'We're not insects are we, Malcolm?' Maggie tugged her brother's sleeve. 'How can we be when we're people?'

'Look.' Malcolm's voice cracked. He placed his arms around his brother and sister and was aware how cold they felt. If only he could light a fire to warm them, bring some joy to this hopeless situation. 'William,' Malcolm said, his voice steadier, 'and all those like him are deluded, they've been brainwashed.'

'Eww, how can you wash a brain?' Tommy screwed up his face again.

Tears burned behind Malcolm's eyes as he managed a weak smile.

'It's just…' Malcolm continued, 'there are people out there who are full of hate, that's all.'

He pulled his brother and sister down onto a rug which was covered in their books and toys.

'We don't hate anyone, do we Tommy?' Maggie sat next to her brother and hugged her knees.

'Only Mrs Bloomberg's dog, he shit in Mummy's laundry basket.'

Maggie giggled. 'Tommy said shit.'

'I know.' Malcolm raised an eyebrow at his brother. 'We don't swear do we, Tommy?'

'I'm sorry, Malcy.' Tommy picked up a wooden car and spun the wheels.

'That's alright, then.' He glanced at the old carriage clock precariously balanced on a wooden crate next to him. Two minutes to five. He stood and made his way over to the trapdoor in the ceiling. A hint of light could be seen around the edges. He listened, willing his heart to stop racing and the footsteps of his mother to grace the floor above.

But there was only silence, other than the ticking of the clock. He took in a long shuddering breath and glanced at the twins who were watching him.

He promised his mother, who had sobbed and sobbed. If she wasn't back by five, she will not be back. Ever. And they will be in danger. They will be found, and they will be killed.

'I guarantee it,' she had told Malcolm, 'I will beg for our lives, I will do whatever it takes, but it may not work, if it doesn't work, it's down to you.'

Malcolm had sat beside his mother on her bed that morning as she explained what she wanted him to do. She was matter of fact about it, but her expression was full of fear.

'But I can fight, Mother,' Malcolm had cried. 'I can fight them all.' Tears streamed down his face in disbelief.

'They will take you away, you and your brother and sister, they will split you up and they will torture you. You must promise me. Promise me, Malcolm Friedmann, that you will do this task. If I am not back at five, then I will be dead.'

Malcolm sobbed as he clutched at his mother. Her stoic composure broke as she tugged him to her and hugged him.

'Five o'clock, remember?' Her voice had been a whisper.

Malcolm watched the hand of the clock move towards the dreaded number. He felt light-headed, his mouth was dry and his heart hammered. He listened again and heard something. Footsteps.

'She's back, oh thank God.' He flicked a look at Tommy and Maggie who were engrossed in their toys.

But the footsteps were heavy, too heavy to be those of his mother, and there was shouting, a lot of shouting, and the thud of furniture being knocked over. He glanced at his siblings; his heart raced. He clenched his fists. It was just a matter of time.

'Come.' His voice cracked as he indicated to his brother and sister. 'Let's eat.'

'What's happening upstairs?' Maggie looked wide-eyed at her big brother. 'I don't like it, it's scaring me.'

'Mummy's made us our favourite drink.' Malcolm's hands shook as he retrieved three cups and a flask from the basket.

'Is it the bad people, Malcy?' Tommy eyes were wide with fear.

'No.' Malcolm's voice was thick. 'Mummy went out to buy new furniture, it's being delivered, that's all.'

Malcolm poured the milky drink into the three cups, spilling some of the contents onto the floor.

'If Fluffy was down here, she'd lick that all up.' Maggie smiled. 'Can we go get Fluffy?'

'No.' Malcolm tried to steady his voice. 'Fluffy's gone to his cousins.'

Maggie looked confused at Tommy who shrugged, nonchalant. 'When I'm older I'm having a dog, cats are so stupid.'

'Fluffy's not stupid, is he Malcy?'

'No.' Malcolm could barely talk. The noise from upstairs was growing, he was running out of time.

'Here.' he handed a cup each to his brother and sister.

'Smells funny,' Maggie wrinkled her nose as she looked at her brother.

'It's alright.' He couldn't do it. He looked up at the trapdoor, and then at the clock, it was now five past five. He *had* to do it; he had no choice. 'It's cinnamon,' he lied. 'Just like we used to get on those nice buns from Mr Glassmann.'

'Do we have buns?' Tommy asked.

Malcolm stared at his little brother and had to stifle a sob. 'After you've finished your drink... yes.'

Tommy smiled, glanced at his sister and gulped down his drink. Maggie did the same.

Malcolm's eyes welled with tears as he watched in horror as his siblings fell to the floor.

'Mummy?' He closed his eyes and mouthed the word silently. 'Mum?'

He heard footsteps above the trapdoor, and a loud harsh voice.

'Open it. Now!'

The cellar walls vibrated from whatever was being used to break open the trapdoor.

Malcolm glanced at his brother and sister, forever asleep. He wiped his eyes and grabbed his cup of 'milk'; his hands trembled as he regarded the lethal creamy contents.

'Quickly!'

He looked up at the trapdoor, barely able to breathe. He was like an animal, trapped with no means of escape.

Then the noise ceased. He let out a long shuddering breath. Maybe they'd gone?

An ear-shattering rattle of machine-gun fire tore apart the silence. The trapdoor bounced open several times.

Malcolm stared at the splintered door unable to move. The trapdoor was yanked back and a face in a black uniform with silver skulls on the jacket collar peered in.

Malcolm took a sip of his drink, he found it wasn't unpleasant.

'In here!'

Two more faces peered down at him. The bad men. The bad men who'd wiped out his family. He gulped the remainder of the liquid and instantly felt as light as air. His throat constricted. He fell to the floor by his brother and sister and reached out to them.

'See you in heaven,' he whispered, as he placed his hands on each of them.

And the cellar went black.

My Cardiff

Eliane Huss

I'll tell you now in a minute
about
My Cardiff
Where the stadium rubs shoulder with the Castle
My Cardiff
Where the salmon jumps up the weir
And the kids slide down
My Cardiff
Where you get stuck in traffic on a magic roundabout
My Cardiff
Where people sing even when they moan
My Home
Capitol to the cwtch, the love spoon and
The mighty Red Dragon.

75 Years Later

Jeff Robson

In the years following the war when all was destroyed
A small group of people sat down together
To say, how shall we be employed?
Writers all they began to know whether
This start-up of CWC would be enjoyed
Over time members found nothing could be better
Than to sit with friends, read, critique and void
The written word they had put to paper, each letter
Was scrutinised, revised, rewritten
After 75 years,
Proof!!

A Private Sea

Sara Hayes

My well-nurtured body
muscle fat bone
is mostly water
salty
a private sea
Washing waves pound my hollow temples
ripple to my sanded nails with every precious beat
of my shaded heart

Somehow
through my skin-bordered wetscape
electricity and other languages
flow
in intimate conversation
I host myriad gossiping floating cells I'll never hear

Life within life
my spirits dance and argue
jostle
fight the beast within
Countless intruders leave in their wake
scars of the battle and weapons for the next

I watch the tides but diaries show the moon can't dictate
when my being cries

tears onto rocks at my
feet
red as the blushing sun
sinking to hide behind the rough stained sea

As I heal again
I sense my innate siren liquid as blackbird's song
escape on breath's mist
beckoning refreshing
waters
to the deep harbour at
my water's edge

The Prince of Abyssinia

Martin Buckridge

Visitors to the quiet church of St Martin's, Bowness-on-Windermere may see the grave of John Bolton, former slave owner and trader, died 21ˢᵗ February 1837. Nearby lies Rasselas Belfield, native of Abyssinia and freed slave, died 16ᵗʰ January 1822.

'Damnation! Another bottle to disturb my sleep, glass everywhere. Have they no respect? I would have them flogged if I could.'

'Men in your employ did a lot of that, Mr Bolton, sir, and more.'

'What! Who speaks? How dare you address me in that manner?'

'Rasselas Belfield, sir. We met last when I was servant to Major Taylor of Belfield House.'

'Ah yes. I recall your impudence, your clothes, too fine for your station and your breeding. It is beyond me why Taylor indulged you so. Damn you.'

'Perhaps, sir, it would be better for you not to use that word beginning with D … especially one in your position.'

'My position? You've lain over there 200 years and I a little less here. The worms consumed us long ago. Bone and dust are all that remains. We are the same in that.'

'It is not bone and dust which will be put in the balance to decide how we shall spend eternity, but our thoughts, words and deeds when we walked among men. In that, sir, we may not be the same.'

'Ha! You remember the parable of the talents in the Book? A master entrusted talents to each of his servants to use wisely while he was away. When the master returned he rewarded the servants who had made profit from the talents and punished the one who had not.'

'I know the story, sir. What of it?'

'I have reflected much on my past and am not free of sin but through my deeds I have lived a life to be commended for industry and achievement.

I, John Bolton, was born humbly near here. At thirteen years I walked alone to Liverpool to work for my uncle. I was quick with numbers and my uncle sent me to the Bluecoat School to study. At sixteen years he found a passage for me to the Windward Isles, to work as apprentice for Rawlinson & Chorley. Ah, I will never forget that first voyage. I landed at St Vincent with nothing but a sack of potatoes on my back and a cheese under my arm. From that beginning I won, lost, and regained my fortunes.'

'How, sir?'

'I worked hard and soon became agent for the company. I borrowed money to buy a few acres and hired slaves to clear ground and plant sugar. Many times I dug alongside them, working as long as they, once nearly dying of the fever. In ten years I amassed ten thousand pounds and returned to Liverpool. In time, I became one of that fair city's largest merchants, employing many. I bought ships to trade and my fortunes grew. I lived as a gentleman, gave much to the needy, even raised 600 men to defend against Napoleon. Later I bought Storrs Hall for my Summer residence. Did you know it?'

'I knew it, sir, a fine house. Once I drove my mistress there to meet with your lady Elizabeth. But tell me, what did you trade on those ships and on how many voyages?'

'I shipped pots, tools, blankets and trinkets to Africa, slaves from Africa to the Caribbean and the Americas, then sugar, tobacco and cotton back to Liverpool. Sixty-nine voyages in all.'

'How many slaves did you take, sir?'

'I do not recall. Yet you are mistaken, I did not take these Africans into slavery. I bought those who were already enslaved by their own kind and merely sold them to the plantations so that they might live productive lives.'

'Productive lives, sir? You sold them for your own enrichment. Were they not chained, branded with their owners' mark and set to work for others?'

191

'It is true, but of necessity. To achieve a greater good some wrongs must often be committed and, the greater the good, the greater the necessary wrong.'

'How can the good have outweighed such wrong, sir?'

'In the first part, these slaves were primitives, children, requiring the discipline of regular work. Was it harsh? Undoubtedly, but a requirement for efficient production and those slaves with strong character understood this. Indeed, I knew freed men who, having worked under the lash, become owners themselves. Sometimes in their hands the lash cut deepest. Would they have done so if they thought it sinful?'

'But, sir, to own men for profit?'

'It is profit that makes the second part. Slavery contributed much to the prosperity of our great nation and without which, I believed, we would all have been much the poorer. My own fortune was the fruit of my labours applying the talents entrusted to me by the Lord, and I did well. Profit allowed me to provide employment and benefit to many. Upon my passing it was written of me that I was one of Liverpool's most honourable merchants and benefactors whom the poor blessed. These were my deeds for the balance and I pray the good will outweigh my sins.'

'Sir, you have used your talents for some public good but I fear the magnitude of your sins may tip the balance to your detriment. By what laws of God and Nature should *you* have owned men like beasts?'

'Now we come to the third part of my reasoning. There have been slaves and owners of all nations on this earth perhaps for as long as man has walked upon it. It may therefore be in the nature of our kind, as God made us, for some to be masters over others.'

'Sir, it cannot be that He set men from one race as being more deserving of slavery than those from another if each race in its turn was both slave and master. The Lord himself said... *as you have done it to one of the least of these my brothers, you have done it to me...* John, was I not your brother and a man?'

'Aye, so you were, Rasselas, and the others too, yet when I lived my eyes did not see it so. But tell me, what of your life as a man?'

'I will tell you. My name was Kaleb, meaning faithful. I was born in Abyssinia, a beautiful wretched land, where tribes made slaves of each other. When famine and disease followed drought, many people sold their children, even themselves. At one such time, when I was eight or nine years, my mother took me to market for the eastern traders to buy. She told me I would be taken to a green land where food would grow on trees and I would never be hungry or cold at night. She gave me her beads as a keepsake saying one day she would find me.'

'And what then?'

'When the traders came my mother held me up and pushed forward, struggling with the crowd to be seen. I was pulled, pinched, measured by many people. Eventually a strange man with eyes the colour of the sky paid my mother and, as he took me, my mother turned to hide her face. I never saw her again.'

'And what of your treatment, Rasselas?'

'You know the man was Major Paul Taylor of the East India Company travelling home from fighting Indian princes. He and his lady were kind. They gave me food, warm clothes, a bed, and I gladly worked in their house. At thirteen years I was baptised as Rasselas, the name for freed men, and welcomed into this church. I learned reading and was instructed in the piano. Major Taylor let me use his library to study philosophy, history, mathematics and poetry. The family were good people and showed me great affection. Belfield became my home, and this, my country.'

'You did well to learn so much, Rasselas. My talents were different and I wish I had your reading. Perhaps one day you will teach me something of the poets? But was there nothing you regret? I remember you strutting like a peacock through town in your fine livery.'

'Yes, the sin of vanity was mine. I was proud of those clothes and to be able to entertain with my music and philosophy. Mostly, I regret those things I did not do. I was loyal to the family but betrayed my birth name. I was unfaithful to my mother whose face and name faded quickly. That I lost her keepsake still breaks my heart. My race, my Abyssinia, I all but forgot. I might have used my talents, to speak and write against the trade like other freed men but did not. It was enough for me to be content in my world.'

'Aye, Rasselas, I have many, many regrets too, but what of Major Taylor, how should he be weighed? The fortune, on which his family lived handsomely, was built on the sale of plantations in South Carolina. They profited from their forebears' slaving. Though Taylor treated you well he bought you as property and took you from your mother. How can *you* say such a man was good?'

'I have no full answer, John, but can speak only for what I know. Over many years the family was acquainted with Mr Wilberforce who rented a house from them. I met him on occasion. Before my birth Mr Wilberforce persuaded the family to sell their plantations. From that time they used their position in the fight against slavery. I remember speaking with many leading abolitionists at Belfield.'

'But, Rasselas, do you think the family's slaving over generations is outweighed by their later abolitionist convictions?'

'I do not know, John, but we are taught that true repentance redeems the soul and perhaps it is true. Yes, I was bought as a slave, but without his wealth and position the Major may not have travelled to an Abyssinian market that day. I would have been taken from my mother by traders and buried a forgotten slave, a single grain in all the sands of Arabia. Instead, I lived in England as a free man and I am grateful.'

'Perhaps Taylor bought you, a black boy, as an adornment for his household as was the fashion?'

'No, John. I was no adornment. Though far from my people I felt like a prince, content, educated and loved as a man. My stone bears testament to the great affection in which I was held... What is written on yours?'

'The facts, no more. My marriage was a cold convenience. We had no children. Friends were companions in business. My eulogies hollow praise from those like myself. I knew little of love.

I wonder sometimes what the living think of me and the world in which we lived. Do you think they judge harshly, Rasselas?'

'They do and with cause. Many visit our graves, yours to condemn and mine to revere. Yet I believe also that one man's judgement of another can sometimes be too harsh if they have not walked his path or looked first to themselves.

You know, John, the living occasionally sit near here to discuss the newspapers. I hear them say that children from Abyssinia are still purchased to work as slaves in these islands. It is known, but they are here. The living say also that the devices they talk into are manufactured using poisonous minerals dug by children from the earth. Everybody has one and cares not. A man tells himself that these things are necessary to his life or that the wealth of nations is dependent on them. When each says the same to the other it becomes true.'

'I hear those conversations too, Rasselas, and they are familiar to me. My conscience was moulded by my own circumstance and I saw only what was convenient. For that I am afraid. But I fear also that it is man's nature to hide from the horrors of this world by retreating to places of comfort and that there is nothing to be done.'

'I hope you are wrong, John, but we must leave affairs of the world to the living. Maybe we can pray together as I believe it may not be too late for us.

But first, let me tell you about Mr Wordsworth. I met him once, you know...'

Time Love and Haiku

Paul Jauregui

in times of nowhen
only emotions between
all ends escaping

love is all
alone this star shines
all is love

through the cold grey dawn
we yearn for solitude's end
finding warmth at last

giving all
each takes their comfort
now is when

Tenby Girl: 1967

Lesley James

In a swimsuit she calls St Clements, stretchy lemon and tangerine with a useless belt, she paddles rock pools, feet wiggling like sepia sea anemones. Next to a starfish, green limpets blurt bubbles; things nibble her toes.

To an audience of kids, men dig out the ice-cream van from the beach. It back-splatters wet cement to escape.

No oil-and-vinegar slick on her today, attracting grit.

Breathe, crushed crab-shells, ice-cream wafers: her mother's stayed at home.

From 2022 to 1947
A Backwards History

A short play by

Sharif Gemie

Performed at the Writers' Gathering on 3rd July 2022
at Jurys Inn Hotel Cardiff

<u>CAST LIST</u>

NICK DUNN A member of 2022 CWC
VIOLET BURMAN Chairman of 1947 CWC
MRS JONES Secretary of the 1947 CWC
MR CHANDLER third member of the 1947 CWC
MISS ROWE fourth member of the 1947 CWC

A FOYER AND A ROOM WITH FIVE CHAIRS: FOUR IN A
ROW, FACING DOWNSTAGE, ONE APART, SLIGHTLY
DOWNSTAGE, FACING STAGE RIGHT. FOUR PEOPLE
SITTING. NICK ENTERS FOYER, STAGE LEFT.

NICK: (NARRATING) I'm late, I know I'm late. They'll have
started without me. Have I got my story, have I got my story?
(CHECKS PHONE) Yes, it's here. Is this the right place?
(LOOKS ROUND—SEES NOTICE) (READS) Cardiff Writers'
Circle—Open Manuscript—All Welcome. Yes, that's it. Right
time? (READS) 3pm, Sunday, 3rd of July. Yes, that's it.

(READS) 1947. (PAUSE) 1947? *1947?*

LOOKS BAFFLED. MOVES TO LEAVE STAGE LEFT, STOPS. TAKES DEEP BREATH, PUSHES HAIR BACK, ENTERS ROOM. ROOM IS ILLUMINATED. THE FOUR PEOPLE SITTING STARE AT NICK.

VIOLET BURMAN: Good afternoon. May I ask your name?

NICK: Nick. (WAVES IN A FRIENDLY WAY TO THE 1947 FOUR.)

VIOLET BURMAN: Nick?

NICK: (NODS)

VIOLET BURMAN: (WITH WEARY PATIENCE) What's your *proper* name?

NICK: Dunn, Nick Dunn.

VIOLET BURMAN: (TO MRS JONES) Were we expecting a Mr Nicholas Dunn?

MRS JONES: (CHECKS NOTES) Yes.

(NICK STARTS IN SURPRISE, FROWNS.)

VIOLET BURMAN: Good afternoon, Mr Dunn. Please sit down. (POINTS TO VACANT CHAIR.)

(NICK SITS.)

VIOLET BURMAN: I am Miss Violet Burman, Madam Chairman of the Cardiff Writers' Circle.

(NICK SNIGGERS AT THE PHRASE '*MADAM CHAIRMAN*', BUT SHE DOESN'T NOTICE.)

VIOLET BURMAN: This is Mrs Jones, Secretary. (MRS JONES NODS AT NICK.) Mr Chandler and Miss Rowe, ordinary members. (THEY SMILE AT NICK.) We'd just been hearing a most interesting article by Mr Chandler concerning a visit to the dentist.

(NICK FACES AUDIENCE AND MOUTHES IN BEWILDERMENT 'A VISIT TO THE DENTIST?')

MRS JONES: I'm sorry, Mr Chandler, but your title's far too long.

MR CHANDLER: Too long, you say?

MRS JONES: (QUOTES) 'The Necessary Preparations for a Dental Visit: Some Recommendations'? (SHAKES HER HEAD.) No, no, no. Popular magazines prefer short, snappy titles, ideally only four or five words long.

MR CHANDLER: Really?

VIOLET BURMAN: The ones which pay best are most demanding.

NICK: (FORGETTING HIMSELF) *Pay?*

(THE FOUR 1947 MEMBERS LOOK AT NICK.)

VIOLET BURMAN: (RESUMING HER TONE OF WEARY PATIENCE) Yes, *pay*. Now that the wartime economy measures have been withdrawn, there's a thriving magazine market out there.

MRS JONES: (HAPPILY) No more paper rationing!

VIOLET BURMAN: They're crying out for copy.

NICK: What are they looking for?

VIOLET BURMAN: Oh, you know, the classic themes. (NICK IS BAFFLED.) Self-improvement, furthering your education. Something that stimulates, (NICK STIFLES A GIGGLE) light romance, beauty and fashion. Nothing too complex.

MR CHANDLER: And war stories.

MRS JONES: (ENTHUSIASTICALLY) My uncle was telling me about Berlin at the end of the war, and how the Russians —

VIOLET BURMAN: (EMPHATICALLY) It's not the easiest of subjects.

MR CHANDLER: (SADLY) No.

(BRIEF PAUSE)

MISS ROWE: Not easy at all. Everyone has a story from the war, but…

(BRIEF PAUSE)

MR CHANDLER: So much destruction. (SHAKES HEAD)

MRS JONES: So many lost friends.

MISS ROWE: So many losses —

VIOLET BURMAN: (EMPHATICALLY) But we're bouncing back. We'll rebuild the bombed cities, we'll create a new, better society.

(MR CHANDLER, MRS JONES AND MISS ROWE STARE AT HER, OBVIOUSLY NOT CONVINCED.)

VIOLET BURMAN: We must look forwards, not backwards.

MR CHANDLER: (SCEPTICALLY) We'll see.

MRS JONES: (SLOWLY, THINKING ALOUD) I suppose that even this little group is a sign that —

VIOLET BURMAN: Exactly! We're doing our bit. Look how we've come on in a just a few months.

MRS JONES: Earning some money, too.

MR CHANDLER: It's not easy, but — (HE SEARCHES FOR WORDS) — there's something strangely satisfying about telling a story, about creating a person and a world. I think I'd call it — (AGAIN, HE SEARCHES FOR THE RIGHT WORD) — *therapeutic.*

(VIOLET BURMAN, MRS JONES AND MISS ROWE NOD IN AGREEMENT.)

VIOLET BURMAN: (THOUGHTFULLY) Yes…

(BRIEF PAUSE AS THE 1947 FOUR LOOK AT EACH OTHER)

NICK: (UNABLE TO STOP HIMSELF, ADDRESSING CHANDLER) But you wrote about going to the dentist!

MR CHANDLER: (LAUGHS) Oh, I was trying to copy what these young ones do. (WINKS AT MRS JONES) Maybe earn a bob or two, as well. What I really want to write is my war memoirs.

MISS ROWE: (TO NICK) Mr Chandler fought in the Western Desert.

MR CHANDLER: And I don't think I'll ever forget it! But how you tell that story… (SHAKES HEAD)

MISS ROWE: (TO MRS JONES) And you were a nurse, weren't you? First in Cardiff, and then sent to France.

MRS JONES: (SHIVERS) I don't think I could write about that. I prefer—I prefer happy stories or romances.

(BRIEF PAUSE)

VIOLET BURMAN: Let's get back to the agenda.

MRS JONES: We need to authorise the subsidy to two members attending the West of England Writers' Conference.

VIOLET BURMAN: That seems straightforward.

NICK: West of *England*?

VIOLET BURMAN: Yes?

NICK: But we're in Wales!

(THE FOUR 1947 MEMBERS STARE AT NICK, THEN LAUGH.)

VIOLET BURMAN: Come now, Cardiff isn't really *Wales*, is it?

(MR CHANDLER, MRS JONES AND MISS ROWE NOD IN AGREEMENT.)

NICK: (DOUBTING HIMSELF) Isn't it? Well — where is Wales?

VIOLET BURMAN: (LAUGHS) Up in the mountains somewhere.

MR CHANDLER: Back in the mists of time — where the dragons live!

(VIOLET BURMAN, MRS JONES AND MISS ROWE LAUGH)

MRS JONES: Mind you, I see some great themes there for travel-writing. It'd make good copy.

MR CHANDLER: Lovely countryside. Let's encourage the day-trippers to visit.

VIOLET BURMAN: Indeed.

MISS ROWE: Maybe Wales is something we could debate one day?

VIOLET BURMAN: Of course. We haven't done much travel-writing yet.

(BRIEF PAUSE)

VIOLET BURMAN: (REMEMBERS NICK AND GIVES HIM A STERN LOOK) Why, what do you write, Mr Dunn?

NICK: (BABBLING WITH ENTHUSIASM, DIAL TURNED UP TO 11) I've just started this cycle about an alternative world that's, like, almost medieval. It's governed by this warrior-elite and there's a rebel prince among them who has this, like, magic gift, a laser sword, but he has a sworn enemy, his half-brother... (THE FOUR 1947 MEMBERS STARE AT HIM, OPEN-MOUTHED. NICK NOTICES THEIR INCREDULITY AND FALLS SILENT.)

(PAUSE)

MRS JONES: I can't see that being published in the *Wrekin Advertiser*.

(THE FOUR 1947 MEMBERS LAUGH.)

NICK: (IRRITATED) I thought you were supposed to be *encouraging* writers.

MISS ROWE: You have to believe in your vision, it's true.

MR CHANDLER: Yes, but—honestly. What next? Elves, wizards, dragons? You'll come here with a three-volume story about a magic ring and a volcano of doom next. (BURMAN AND JONES SMILE AND SHAKE THEIR HEADS.) We've got to be realistic.

MRS JONES: You have to cut your cloth to suit your coat.

VIOLET BURMAN: (WITH ONE EYE ON THE MRS JONES—MRS JONES FOLLOWS HER WORDS, RUNS A PEN ALONG HER NOTES, AND NODS IN CONFIRMATION AT EACH ITEM) So far today, we've agreed on arrangements for the Christmas dinner. Mrs Jones has entertained us with her short story 'Poppy Day' and her poem 'Winter Lights.' I have contributed an article on 'Picking Yourself Up', for which Mrs Jones was good enough to suggest several possible publications. I think we're all agreed that while Mr Chandler's article has possibilities, it's not quite ready for publication. (MR CHANDLER SIGHS IN A GOOD-HUMOURED WAY, NODS.) We've accepted the subsidy for the delegates to the West of England Conference. (SHE GLANCES AT NICK, EXPECTING DISAGREEMENT.) As we only have three minutes left, I think it would be best if we conclude… (HER VOICE FADES AS NICK SPEAKS.)

(NICK STANDS UP AND ADDRESSES THE AUDIENCE.)

NICK: This isn't what I expected. They're all so stuffy and formal. They won't like what I want to write about—I don't feel like reading anything to this crowd. All they think about is selling what they write! (LOOKS EXASPERATED, THEN RE-THINKS.) Mind you—it would be nice to be paid for writing. Could that ever happen to me? (PAUSE. NICK SHAKES HIS HEAD) Is this *Creative Writing*? What happened to living your dream?

(BEHIND NICK, VIOLET BURMAN, MRS JONES AND MR CHANDLER START PACKING PAPERS INTO BRIEFCASES, PUTTING ON THEIR COATS, AND GIVING EVERY SIGN OF BEING ABOUT TO LEAVE. MISS ROWE STAYS IN HER CHAIR. SHE LOOKS INCREASINGLY AGITATED.)

MISS ROWE: Madam Chairman?

(VIOLET BURMAN IGNORES HER.)

MISS ROWE: (MORE LOUDLY) Madam Chairman?

VIOLET BURMAN: Yes?

MISS ROWE: I signalled at the start of the meeting that I have something to read today.

VIOLET BURMAN: (LOOKS AWKWARD, THEN OSTENTATIOUSLY CHECKS HER WATCH.) Beaten by the clock, Miss Rowe.

(PAUSE. VIOLET BURMAN AND MISS ROWE STARE AT EACH OTHER.)

MISS ROWE: Now look here. I can't speak at my church, because that's the vicar's job. I can't speak out at my school, because a schoolmistress has to do what the headmaster tells her. But I'll be *damned* (VIOLET BURMAN, MRS JONES AND MR CHANDLER FLINCH) if I stay silent here.

(PAUSE. VIOLET BURMAN, MRS JONES AND MR CHANDLER EXCHANGE GLANCES. NICK IS AMAZED.)

VIOLET BURMAN: (SIGHS) Well, if that's the way you feel. (SIGNALS TO MRS JONES AND MR CHANDLER. THEY SIT BACK IN THEIR CHAIRS.)

MISS ROWE: (SARCASTICALLY, COOLLY) Thank you.

(MISS ROWE STANDS UP. SHE OPENS A NOTEBOOK, FLICKS THROUGH THE PAGES.)

MISS ROWE: This is a poem about transience, it's for someone — someone I once knew.

(VIOLET BURMAN NODS AND SMILES IN A PATRONISING MANNER. MRS JONES AND MR CHANDLER ASSUME SELF-CONCIOUSLY 'LISTENING' POSES. NICK IS BEWILDERED, BUT CLEARLY DOESN'T EXPECT MUCH FROM MISS ROWE.)

MISS ROWE: (ADDRESSES AUDIENCE. AS SHE READS,
HER VOICE GROWS STRONGER. THE FOUR
LISTENERS — INCLUDING NICK — GROW FASCINATED.)

The Guardians

Give me your hands to hold

I knew them once, pliant and beautiful,
Their touch like snow-cooled water
To a traveller's thirst. Long since
I knew them thus, and lightly used them,
Nor guessed that through the years,
They would be always waiting to receive
My gifts, nor ever to refuse

No longer are they pliant,
Withered and gnarled and dry, they stubbornly
Guard still the sorrows and the shame
With which I burdened them.
Open them now, no longer hide
From the world's eye these hateful things.
Uncup your hands.

Empty? Where then
Are the old knotted sins,
The shabby subterfuge, the shame?
What have you wrought on them
That they have not endured?
Oh! if Time keeps for us yet
A few short years to share,
Then, while we live —

Give me your hands to hold.

(PAUSE)

NICK: (TO AUDIENCE) Wow!

(ALL FOUR CLAP.)

END

Jam Machine

Richard Prygodzicz

Prodding the machine, he remembered they pressed something for the flap to open before the teletubbys appeared. His free hand pushed a button. The tray whirred.

He pressed, repeatedly. WWHHRR! WWHHRR! WWHHRR! Entranced by sound and movement.

From his stroller, biting his toast, he wondered… did the box need feeding?

Looking at the opened tray, then behind, ensuring he was alone, and finally to his toast. A smile appeared.

'Micky, what have you done… again?' Mam said.

Descriptions of the contributing writing groups

Cardiff Writers' Circle aims to foster the art of writing in all its forms, to give help and guidance to members, especially those writing for publication, and to provide a welcoming and inclusive meeting ground for all those interested in writing. We meet every Monday evening and welcome adults from all backgrounds. Our usual base is the YMCA in Shakespeare Street off City Road but since the Covid crisis some meetings are held by Zoom. Most meetings are 'open manuscript' in which members at all stages of development read from their own work and receive constructive feedback, with no censorship. Meetings are safe spaces for members. CWC holds six annual competitions: short story, poetry, flash fiction, article/review, and two for short humorous pieces. We published *Write on Cardiff*, our first anthology, in 2019 and early in 2021 ran a successful series of short story writing workshops led by Mab Jones for our members. The workshops were generously supported by Literature Wales.

Cardiff University Creative Writing Society is a supportive and social group for students at Cardiff University. As well as feedback sessions, it holds educational events and offers opportunities for members to have their work published. There's also a chance to be part of a wider student community and new members are welcomed, often via an ice cream parlour.

Roath Writers aims to be a welcoming space for writers of all levels to write, develop, and share their work in an informal environment. Members will read and discuss a piece of published poetry or prose, write something new and have a chance to read their writing in every session. We always head to the pub afterwards where lively discussion sparked by books, films, poetry, and literary events is also encouraged!

Tuesday Night Writes currently meets online on the first Tuesday of the month. You can find us on Facebook, search for Tuesday Night Writes (HOME). We're a small group who have traditionally specialised in script writing; before the pandemic, we produced annual scratch nights at The Gate, showcasing our work. More recently, members have branched out into short stories and novels. The work displayed here is a good representation of individual's interests and styles.

Write On! with Alix creative writing classes for women:
Ever wanted to write? Looking for creative inspiration or a place to share your thoughts in a safe non-judgemental space? Your skill level doesn't matter. Whether you write regularly, sometimes journal, or never write anything except a shopping list, this class is for you.

This group was set up by Cardiff Women's Centre and Alix Edwards, writer, artist and founder of Company of Words spoken word events, to provide a safe space for women of all abilities to explore creative writing. This class is open to all women. All resources are provided. Suitable for experienced writers as well as those who are new to writing.

The event is hosted by Cardiff Women's Aid and meets Wednesdays 1.30-3.30pm.

To find out more please email
SHOUT@cardiffwomensaid.org.uk or call 02920 460566

Author Biographies

Saoirse Anton is an Irish writer, theatremaker, producer, critic. She is a feminist, optimist, enthusiast, opinionated scamp. Her poetry has been published in *Rise Up and Repeal*, a Sad Press Poetry anthology. She is working on her debut album and pamphlet. She performs her work extensively in Ireland and the UK.

Jade Bangs: I've been writing fantasy stories for as long as I can remember. I'm based in Kent, though I'm studying Ancient History in Cardiff, and have fallen in love with the place. I am currently working on my own novel, particularly inspired by Persian mythology.

Martin Buckridge was born in Peru but lived most of his childhood in West Kirby on the Wirral. Now mainly retired, he had a career in museums, industrial archaeology, and grant giving. He is married and lives in Cardiff. A relative newcomer to creative writing, Martin produces short stories and poetry.

Pamela Cartlidge was born in north Wales. She moved to Cardiff in 2001 where she began researching for the novel she'd always wanted to write. After the death of her mother, she published *Bluebells and Tin Hats*, inspired by events in her family during the nineteen thirties and forties.

Nejra Ćehić is a poet and short story writer, currently working on her first novel. She was born in Sarajevo and moved to Cardiff when she was seven, living there until the age of eighteen. She currently lives in France with her partner and one-year-old daughter.

A.H. Creed is a best-sulking author currently working on a debut novel described as: *what you'd get if James Herriot and Eleanor Oliphant had a baby.* Previously published by people old enough to know better, A.H. has also been charged with aiding and abetting the publication of others.

Nick Dunn, a subspecies of nomadic Englishman once thought extinct, was discovered to have been living in Wales since 2010. Known only as "Nick Dunn", the long-haired creature is rarely seen in the wild. If stumbled upon, it can be placated with chocolate biscuits and the promise of books.

Denise Dyer was born and raised in Cardiff. She's travelled extensively and has an interest in nature and ancient history. Life got in the way of her writing until recently when she attended a creative writing class that nurtured her fertile imagination, dark humour, and variable style of writing.

Alix Edwards is a multi-platform artist and facilitator. She uses painting, photography and spoken word to tell untold stories about loss, resilience and shame. Her mission is to empower others through their own creativity. She is part of 2022-23 Representing Wales cohort (Literature Wales) and has exhibited work in the UK, Barcelona and LA.

Angela Edwards was born in Kent, worked in London in adoption and residential work, then moved to a Welsh smallholding with husband and children before finally settling in Cardiff. She has been published in anthologies and magazines, including *The New Welsh Review*, and the York Poetry Society, and self-published two poetry collections; *A Rose in Snow* and *If Fire Could Be Blue*.

Eryl Samuels lives near Cardiff where he was born and brought up. He was shortlisted for the Rhys Davies Short Story Competition in 2022. A collection of his short stories, *Words are Like Birds*, was published in 2021. He has also written a novel, *Cat's Eyes*, published in 2020.

Morgan Fackrell is a dabbler in the mystic art of writing, sporadically returning to write poetry ensuring she does not adhere to any of the usual conventions or rules. Her comfort zone is speculative/science fiction. Currently working on a contemporary novel of love, friendship, trauma and redemption within a lesbian community.

Peter Gaskell: Awarded a Masters degree in Scriptwriting with distinction in 2014, I've been recently focusing on prose fiction, taking encouragement from an agent for a novel I put on authonomy.com. Furthermore, I took runner-up and 'highly commended' credits from Writers Forum magazine competitions for my short stories which make me hopeful of publication too.

Sharif Gemie is a happily retired historian who took up Creative Writing five years ago. His first novel, *The Displaced*, will be published in April 2023: it's about a middle-class British couple who volunteer to work with refugees in Germany at the end of the Second World War.

Malaysian-born **Nisha Harichandran** embraced her creative wings after a fifteen-year legal career in Asia and Europe in an operational and strategic role. Now, as a writer and JOY coach, she's enjoying life in Cardiff and fulfilling her purpose of working with people to have a positive impact on themselves.

Sara Hayes has written for fun for a very long time. Since retiring, she has joined Cardiff Writers' Circle, which is even more fun. She has had one poem published and many poems and short stories rejected. She is working on a historical novel set in China at the birth of the Empire.

Ruth Hogger joined Cardiff Writers' Circle when she moved to Cardiff from Ireland in 2019. She has been the recipient of the Circle's Hilda McKenzie short story trophy twice. She works as an online therapist and loves to write to explore folklore and the depths of human emotion.

Originally from Luxembourg, a whirlwind and nomad in her youth, **Eliane Huss** settled in Cardiff twenty-six years ago and raised two fine sons. A true survivor of life, she has taken up writing to share her stories and thoughts and of course have some fun doing so.

Lesley James's chapbook *Walk with Scissors* is published by Infinity Books. Other publications: *Spelt, Broken Spine, BSAC05, Best of Café Lit 2022, Love the Words Dylan Thomas Anthology, Full House LitMag* and *Roi Fainéant*. Shortlisted for LoveReadingUK's Very Short Story Award 2022. Children's poetry: *Dirigible Balloon, Parakeet, Chasing Clouds Anthology.*

All his life **Paul Jauregui** has had stories battering around in his head, screaming to be released. His previous audience of two daughters escaped, but he now has two grandchildren who are too little to do that. Yet. He only became chair of Cardiff Writers' Circle to gain a captive audience.

Jane King: I write poetry, short stories and plays. A few have been published and most haven't. My play *The Pier End* was performed on Penarth Pier in August 2022. I'm left-handed, imaginative and creative (I once knitted a piano). I have taught Science, Drama and Life Skills and have run two successful businesses. GSOH.

Leusa Lloyd is a journalist who works in broadcast television. After spending her teenage years writing poetry, she has finally decided to unleash some of her writing on the world and is seeking publishing opportunities. She has recently begun writing short stories and is attempting her first novel.

Paul Mackay was born in Antwerp, Belgium to British Service personnel. After a childhood spent living and experiencing different regions across the UK and Europe, he finally settled in Cardiff, where he has written for both theatre and TV, as well as producing and directing staged festival events.

Sarah Mayo had a writer's disposition even before she fully immersed herself in creative writing just a few years ago. Born in Aberdare, she loves the fact she is from the town once described as 'The Athens of South Wales'. Writing is her catharsis, an unrelenting pursuit of a 'sweet release.'

Ian McNaughton, has-been chef and writer from Cardiff, pens short humorous stories with a subtle food twist. Although he holds a Certificate of Higher Education in creative writing from Cardiff University, his rejections still outweigh his publications. He always has to look up how to spell broccolli. Ian can be found at cardiffstoryweaver.com

Patty Papageorgiou began writing stories at an early age until the magic of cinema lured her into pursuing that side of the craft. She has held various production roles in the UK Film & TV industry before focusing exclusively on screenwriting in 2017. She freelances as a script editor and analyst, while writing her own material.

Stephen Pritchard is married with two children and five grandchildren. He is Emeritus Librarian, Cardiff University and formerly: Director of Information Services, University of Wales College of Medicine; Staff Coach (Middle Distance Events) for Athletics Wales, Senior Coach with GB Athletics and former chair of Cardiff Writers' Circle.

Richard Prygodzicz writes for children, mainly picture books and middle grade novels, under the pen name Jerzy Jones. Writing, off and on, for over thirty years, Jerzy decided to self-publish during 2020 having been told, by people in the writing industry, that his work was good enough to be published. 'Growing children's imagination' is his main aim.

Pip Pryor: I am a non-binary writer currently studying English Literature & Creative Writing at Cardiff University and a member of their Creative Writing Society. Due to my studies, I am based in both Cardiff and Milton Keynes. A lot of my work explores gender and sexuality outside of the heteronormative expectation, influenced by my own experiences.

Jeff Robson joined Cardiff Writers' Circle in 2016. Since then he has written 350 poems and twenty-five short stories. He has taken part in every in-house competition, winning a number of them and was featured five times in the last compilation of 2019. Serving presently as treasurer.

Sharha is a Kamasutra Feminist and a Doctoral Researcher at Cardiff Metropolitan University. She is refiguring an ancient text *The Kamasutra* for making modern women empowered and discovering gender equality in terms of pleasure. She has three creative writing publications. Currently, she is working to introduce Kamasutra Feminism through her doctoral thesis.

Suzanne Shepherd is a busy mother and grandmother working in a Cardiff High School. She studied law, graduating in 2015, and has been a magistrate. She has had the pleasure of fostering nearly 200 children over nineteen years. She relishes keeping active. Most of all though, she enjoys her family time.

Jacqueline L Swift lives in the Vale of Glamorgan. She ran her own photography business for eighteen years before turning to her first love, writing. She has successfully written for stage and screen and is now writing her first novel set during the aftermath of World War Two.

Dave Thomas is a part-time sweet cone manufacturer and lawn-mower salesman. He writes principally to amuse his kids and annoy his wife. He is an irregular on the Sharm-El-Sheikh comedy circuit, where he hones his open mic skills to mostly bewildered silence. He is a member of Cardiff Writers' Circle, where he is currently banned from reading any more poetry. [Ed: Not true]

I'm **Katherine Wheeler** and my name is a pun. I'm a student at Cardiff University, but more importantly I'm a writer, editor and zine publisher. My current work explores sci-fi and body horror, drawing inspiration from Nemo Ramjet's *All Tomorrows* and Ted Chiang to create a delicious atmosphere of all-consuming dread.

Originally from the East Midlands, **Jennifer Wilkinson** has lived more than half her life in south Wales. She's written many short stories and scripts and has had a few published or performed. She has a completed novel, ready to submit to agents and is editing a second one.

Alexander Winter is a Cardiff-based writer, having found his way there through a Creative Writing BA at Aberystwyth. He is a frequent attendee of Roath Writers and has just completed the Creative Writing MA at Cardiff University. He has a wife, three cats and far too many hobbies.

On Our Seventy-Fifth Anniversary
Let Us Now Praise
the Unknown Writer

Stephen Pritchard

The Unknown Writer represents all those members of Cardiff Writers' Circle whose existence is unrecorded in the Circle's written histories, minutes, list of Officers and whose name has never appeared on the Roll of competition winners.

Yet for seventy-five years the Unknown Writer's readings and feedback have been the Circle's unacknowledged life blood, sustaining its very existence, week after week, decade after decade.

When the captains and the kings depart, the Unknown Writer will remain.

Cardiff 75
Contemporary writing
from the city

Some collections serve to mark particular events or milestones, whilst others contain work of the highest quality. This collection manages both of these things, with 75 pieces of poetry and short fiction by local writers celebrating 75 years of creative writing in this fabulous city of the arts.

Cardiff Writers' Circle was formed in 1947 and is joined here by other local writing groups, all lending their imaginations to a wide variety of styles, genres, and formats. You may laugh. You may cry. You may gasp at the sheer beauty contained within these pages. But above all, you will be holding a snapshot of the fantastic talent that exists today in Cardiff, city of the dragon.

This publication has been supported by

PARTHIAN

Viridor and
Prosiect Gwyrdd
Community Fund

PARTHIAN

CREE:
THE RHYS DAVIES SHORT
STORY AWARD ANTHOLOGY

Edited by Elaine Canning

A collection of new contemporary short
stories by Welsh writers, representing
the winners of the 2022 Rhys Davies
Short Story Competition

PB / £10.00
978-1-914595-23-3

AN OPEN DOOR:
NEW TRAVEL WRITING FOR A
PRECARIOUS CENTURY

Edited by Steven Lovatt

"thoughtful, passionate and sensitive to
both the similarities and differences of
non-domestic cultures" – Noel Gardner,
Buzz Magazine

PB / £10.00
978-1-913640-62-0

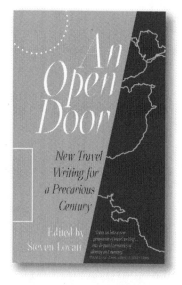